ARRIVING IN AVIGNON

ARRIVING IN AVIGNON

A RECORD

DANIËL ROBBERECHTS
TRANSLATED BY PAUL VINCENT

DALKEY ARCHIVE PRESS
CHAMPAIGN AND LONDON

Originally published in Flemish as *Aankomen in Avignon* by Uitgeverij Manteau, 1970

Library of Congress Cataloging-in-Publication Data

Robberechts, Daniël.
[Aankomen in Avignon. English]
Arriving in Avignon / Daniël Robberechts ; translated by Paul Vincent. -- 1st ed.
   p. cm.
Originally published in 1970 in Flemish as Aankomen in Avignon.
ISBN 978-1-56478-592-3 (pbk. : alk. paper)
1. Young men--France--Fiction. 2. Avignon (France)--Fiction. 3. Psychological fiction. 4.
Autobiographical fiction. I. Vincent, Paul (Paul F.) II. Title.
PT6466.28.O2A6513 1010
839.31'364--dc22
                         2010022648

Partially funded by the University of Illinois at Urbana-Champaign and by a grant from the
Illinois Arts Council, a state agency

The translation of this book is funded by the Flemish Literature Fund (Vlaams Fonds voor
de Letteren—www.flemishliterature.be)

www.dalkeyarchive.com

Cover: design and composition by Danielle Dutton, illustration by Nicholas Motte
Printed on permanent/durable acid-free paper and bound in the United States of America

When Daniël Robberechts took his life in 1992, he was fifty-five years old, and the author of nine books. The first two were published in 1968, but only his debut—*De labiele stilte* (The Unstable Silence)—could be described as adhering to the conventions of literary fiction. This practice was quickly abandoned—the practice, that is, of inventing characters to be described and exploited in the hope of netting a reader's empathy en route—with Robberechts focusing his attentions on a construct perhaps no less artificial, but holding, he saw, a great deal more potential, and necessitating little or no manipulation or mendacity: Daniël Robberechts, and the wider world he inhabited.

Arriving in Avignon (1970), labeled not a novel but "a record," sees the author mastering an uneasy synthesis between fiction and journal, confession and travel guide. It could be mistaken for a fragmentary coming of age novel if it wasn't for the fact that the narrator seems, by the final pages, to have advanced no further than a state of permanent, if melancholy, adolescence. It might be mistaken for a *bildungsroman* if the narrator's education didn't prove so entirely pyrrhic: sex immolates every opportunity he has to see what really goes on around him; and then, as an adult, writing in settled, lettered, literary retrospect, we find the writer trying and failing to bury his undiminished lust and discontent under facts, names, dates, history—his own, and that of a city that had never much interested him.

Arriving has been described as a one-man siege, with the ancient, walled city of Avignon standing in for the many things the young narrator does and does not want to attain, to arrive into: maturity, independence, marriage, stability. If we must read the city symbolically, however, it might be more to the point—and closer to Robberechts's philosophy—to see Avignon as that "thing" which writing can never wholly capture . . . that is to say, *everything* we experience: everything unwritten. Robberechts can never arrive in Avignon. When he walked through its streets as a young man, he couldn't see it—it didn't register. Now, at his desk, writing about it, all he can see are words and women (and the occasional man). No wonder then that the author's next "record," *Praag schrijven* (Writing Prague, 1975), saw Robberechts laying siege to a city he had never even visited.

Words turn everything into fiction, of course. It is Robberechts's triumph that—with a bit of a smirk, never quite believing in his "imprecise . . . naïve . . . ill-considered" project—he manages, here, to build a city and consciousness into which *we*, as readers, can fully arrive.

Beginning on page 141, this edition of Arriving in Avignon *includes Daniël Robberechts's collection of the original foreign-language quotations employed in writing the text.*

ARRIVING IN AVIGNON

In the diary that he has kept since he was eighteen, the name of the town is mentioned explicitly at least ten times within a period of four years. An investigation of the routes that he probably followed on the various journeys documented in the same diary and spread over eight years, including the above-mentioned four, leads one, moreover, to the conclusion that he must have got into or out of a train in that town's station, or else must have traveled through that station on a train, or traveled in some other vehicle through or around the edge of that town, about twenty times. These are facts and figures that are difficult to argue with, and yet it's quite possible that he'll none-theless maintain that Avignon means little or nothing to him. In response to that one should say that he ought to know better; that it is unlikely at best for someone who is not a professional traveler "just happening" "with impunity" to be repeatedly in the same place, about nine hundred kilometers from his hometown, on average three or perhaps four times a year over a period of eight years, and whose view of that place, because of his various visits, their dates often falling outside the usual holiday periods, must of course have differed considerably from that of those tourists for whom this town is just the first leg of a trip through the South of France, and then too from that of the vacationers who stop in at the town on their way to the Mediterranean coast and are only urged on to greater haste by all its southern features; and given, finally, that Avignon, though primarily a transit hub, has none of the cosmopolitan neutrality of other such cities—for instance, Paris, which he had to pass through whenever he traveled by rail—that it is, again, unlikely at best for someone like him, and a northerner to boot, to be so often in the same town and have it make no impression upon him. Alternatively, one could ask him curtly: Have you been to the town or not, yes or no?—"Of course I have."—On more than one occasion?—"Definitely."—Including at times of the year that for most of us would be unusual?—"Certainly." Though actually, the main thing is to get him to accept that his experience of Avignon as an essentially arbitrary town (which could thus be replaced either by Prague, a town he's never set foot in, or indeed by his hometown) and perhaps even as an arbitrary object (just not so central an object, so exclusively personal, that any statement about it would become problematic)—however fragmentary and unsystematic this experience, however inadequate for a historian, a geographer, an economist, a sociologist, an archaeologist, a compiler of travel guides, or even a tourist—precisely because of its randomness, its physical, synthetic innocence, offers the chance of an exploration, of course lacking the thoroughness of a scientific research project, but being therefore a report that would have room for everything that scientists must neglect for the sake of objectivity: an ordinary human statement that might satisfy in us precisely what all scientific literature fails to satisfy.

And then it turns out that his very first contact with the town on the Rhone (apart from a purely verbal one, when as a toddler he had learned to sing the dance tune that goes: *Sur le pont / d'Avignon / on y danse, on y danse / sur le pont d'Avignon / on y danse tous en rond*—and it was only recently that he'd heard that the lyrics originally went <u>*Sous*</u> *le pont d'Avignon*, when the *Pont Saint-Bénezet* still spanned the river and people crossed in the shadow of its arches to dance on the *île de la Barthelasse*) actually predates the earliest entries in the preserved diary by several years: He was fourteen, and the first and ultimately last full-force family trip in the first post-war car through Southwest France and Northern Spain had been interrupted at the start of the return journey in the village of Remoulins (near *Pont-du-Gard* on the right bank of the Rhone) by a breakdown requiring the replacement of parts that in the France of the time were obtainable only in Paris; for him, however, since he had passed the entrance exam to an insane asylum masquerading as an officers' training academy where the academic year began earlier than elsewhere, a speedy return to Brussels was required, so it was decided that he would travel home with his mother by train, his older brother accompanying them as far as Paris, while the father, sister, and younger brother would stay in Remoulins. That's as far as the anecdote goes. But what does it mean to a boy who one autumn day drives for the first time—in a coach rather than a taxi? or in the garage-owner's car? he has forgotten—over the *Pont Saint-Pierre* across the Rhone to Avignon Station? Well, he's fourteen. Up till then he was a definitely non-brilliant pupil at a Jesuit college, he's a patrol leader in a scout troop; he doesn't yet wear glasses; he's taller than the other boys in his class; in Spain he wore shorts, his older brother ordinary long trousers; up till now he has smoked few if any cigarettes. An adolescent? Nowhere near. Preadolescent? In any case, less likely then to find himself in crisis, less likely at the very least to find himself beset by bewildering fantasies or disturbing questions than in the previous two years. He still wears his hair parted on the left, which gives him a smart, respectable look. He's also still an absolute virgin. For quite some time there's been an unusual lack of intimacy in his relationship with his housemates; in fact he has no friendships to speak of, and since he doesn't belong to a single natural, freeform group of adolescents, he cannot compare himself with any of his peers. Is there anything more awkward than wasting words on such a solitary, vague individual? It's as if each word is harshly, overbearingly imposing its form on something that is of course formless. Perhaps one should express it like this: appearance and strength almost those of a man, but a skin, a heart, a brain like a child's—or perhaps a girl's? Facts. On the way there he got drunk for the first time with his older brother in Fontainebleau, and he's very proud that no one in the *Hôtel de l'Aigle Noir* noticed a thing. In the last months of the school year, almost every morning, in the empty Ursulinenstraat on his way to school Mass, he met a girl with long straight hair who clutched her schoolbag to her bosom like a tiny lover—and he felt an astonishment that was new, and impressive, not just his earlier vague curiosity. In Périgueux he drank rosé wine for the first time, and laughed with the others because his father was slightly tipsy, or acted as if he was. On the beach in Biarritz he was fascinated by a dark-blue bathing suit—and was it for that reason and at that time that his sister, who is the eldest, praised his good taste? In San Sebastián or Pamplona a bullfight left him cold, perhaps his revulsion was all channeled into his contempt for the picador. In Tudela he gaped at the gold plate of a Spanish church during Sunday Mass. In the empty *Gran Hotel* in Saragossa he made an attempt to strike up a conversation with a bellboy of his age or slightly younger, whom he found attractive? pretty? likeable?, and offered him something—a cigarette?—but neither of them found a viable means of verbal communication, and when the presence of his older brother behind him became too much for him, and behind the bellboy a smarmy, hurried, plump grownup member of the hotel staff approached as if trying to avert a disaster with a smile, and he saw in the way the other boy looked at the waiter a helpless readiness to conform unconditionally to the norms of the grownups, and the cigarette was refused—the approach foundered, and humiliated by the meekness of the other boy, he bit his lip, and the deeply blushing prince resolved never again to embarrass his subjects by infringing upon etiquette. Barcelona, and the cyclopean cliffs of Montserrat. Did he tell his sister anything about the very young blonde girl in Lloret? (Lloret with at most three hotels, including one—theirs—where the roof leaked; where in the mornings before ten o'clock you saw no one under the palms on the promenade except children with their black-and-white uniformed nannies; where in the tent close to the high-tide mark deadly serious children of ten congregated to dance.) It's not impossible that he joked with his sister and younger brother about being in love during the days they spent lying on the beach eating small, very sweet grapes: joking, although painful, was still at least talking about her, using words to describe her; and what else could he do? When she frolicked in the sand with her Spanish boyfriends, he felt like a stuffy furtive old voyeur ogling young girls, and in the evenings when she danced he could only look, peep longingly, he couldn't dance, but talking to her was impossible, smiling at her, touching her unthinkable; not even—and how much he would have liked to do so—the evening she started to cry for some reason he couldn't guess, and left the dance tent for the only movie theater in town where for hours he divided his attention between her shadow and a noisy and probably stupid Mexican comedy, of which he understood not a word: condemned, provisional, *extranjero*, or worse still: *turista*. This is the immediate past that this overgrown boy brings with him if not into Avignon, then over the Rhone. Shortly he will try in vain to make his helpless passion for the girl of Lloret degenerate into doggerel. In eight years' time he will basically not behave any differently towards the student Christiane than he did with the girl in Lloret: a beggar, a plague victim perhaps who doesn't dare enter the town gate until someone extends a hand to conduct him in. He will never say anything to his sister about the morning girl-in-Ursulinenstraat whom he will never meet again. It will be another ten years before he acknowledges that her whole attitude was receptive, expectant, compliant, and that the girl in Lloret probably flirted with him too, more or less unconsciously. During future holidays he won't so much as open his mouth at home—even now he avoids mentioning school. The boys in his dormitory will prove no more approachable than the bellboy from the *Gran Hotel*, although he will once and for all adopt their language, Flemish, as his own. Everything will happen there as if from the very first days a hunched, frozen, shivering war orphan, eyes wide with fear, were hiding inside his strapping body, always far too terrified to understand what's happening to him. When in six years' time he decides to run away from the "insane asylum," the sanctuary he plans on will not be his family's Brussels mansion—he will apply for a visa for Spain; and it won't be a housemate who persuades him at the last moment to flee in a less adventurous way. Between this as yet unsuspected, life-changing future, which will descend upon him like a supernatural vocation, which will pounce upon him like a disaster, and then his harmless past, like one long holiday: the town of Avignon? But even if he really did enter the town at this time, on the way to the "asylum," it's basically as though after crossing the bridge he drove immediately down the *Boulevard de l'Oulle,* the *Boulevard Saint-Dominique,* and the *Boulevard d'Estienne d'Orves,* right to the station. In that case he must have looked at the smooth, surprisingly clean, almost white walls, but it's not certain that they inspired any feelings in him other than a memory of the wooden toy castle, with battlements, keep, and drawbridge, in which, not so long ago, he could arrange only anachronistic tin or plaster soldiers. Because this very first real movement in the direction of Avignon is dominated—even more so than by innocent curiosity about the "asylum"—by excitement at the prospect of his first journey on an express. The very fact that that train had its own name gave it the glamour of an *Orient Express,* a *Trans-Siberian.* Even before he could attach any meaning to the fact that the name of the northwesterly wind that the express had been given was also that of a great poet (many of whose works first appeared in Avignon), that association of train and wind (*Faster-than-the-Wind* was the name of a character from a children's book his father had once given him) was bound to make the experience of any journey on the *Mistral* into an event. Perhaps it would have been a disappointment to observe that the train that pulled into the station was actually no different from other trains—the *Mistral* was probably still pulled by a steam engine at that time, at least until it reached Lyon—if one's attention had not been distracted by the excitement of boarding, the suitcases that mustn't be forgotten, the reserved seat that one must find, his mother's alarm, the jostling, the noise. And even after the train had left, it would have been disappointing to note that one felt little of the celebrated top speeds as printed in the train corridor next to the map of France, but then the prospect of his first visit to a restaurant car was sufficient to keep up the suspense. So his very first move in the direction of Avignon turns out ultimately to have been a move *away* from Avignon. Just as a spiral never truly turns in upon its center, but at each point is always a little less perpendicular to its origin than the circumference drawn through that point.

Avignon, September 29, 1843 . . . The district that I am now traversing is very fine . . . it is impossible to find a country more nearly resembling Spain. There is the same aspect of town and landscape; the workmen lie in the shade and drop their cloaks with a tragic air that is Andalusian; the odor of garlic and oil is mingled with that of oranges and jasmine; the streets are shaded with linen during the day, and the women have small, well-shod feet; there is nothing, even to the patois, that has not a flavor of Spain. A still closer relation exists in its abundance of gnats, fleas, and other insects, making sleep impossible . . . This is from Mérimée's *Letters to an Incognita*, a two-volume book, of which he was given a secondhand copy bought in England by his younger brother. But more than his memories of Spain, it will be two Greek journeys that decisively win him over to the country into which Avignon gives access. Ionic or Doric columns, new names (Nauplia, Mykene, Bassai, Athene, Rhodos,

Andritsaina, and also Charilao or Charitheo, borne by a mule-driver), traveling companions (the unattainable girl Kitty; the memory of ambiguous expressions of affection on the part of an American cabin companion on the SS *Barletta*, which he, however unconsciously, had answered no less ambiguously now generating the same unease as the Hermes of Praxiteles in the cramped space of the museum at Olympia), shrines with very un-Classical, gruesome origins (fatal Eleusinian Mysteries, panic-striking thunderstorms above the Delphic chaos, human sacrifices demanded by Olympian Hera)—ultimately this revelation is satisfyingly subsumed in the poetic contemplation of olives and cypresses. There is a decisive moment when he—an up-and-coming youth of seventeen who combs his hair back and whose beard is starting to grow? in the corridor of a train out of Salonica?—looks out of the window at the break of day. He did not know, still doesn't know if the train had already passed Avignon, and whether the hills or mountains, behind whose inky black bulk the multicolored light rose even more gloriously, were called *les Alpilles* or *les Baronnies*, but he saw that there beyond the train window the same silence reigned and the same light—I must come back here, he decided—the same light and the same silence as in the early morning of August 2, 1954, quite a while before dawn, when the engines had fallen silent, and when he got up on deck he saw that the ship was scraping its way between two tall, almost vertical cliffs, from the fore-deck one could see the chugging tug out ahead; then the tall cliffs dropped away, cables were paid out, the tugboat continued by itself in a wide arc, and as the deck slid past the cliff he felt as though he were being pushed face-down into a pillow of aromas that he would only afterward be able to label as resin and thyme, it was suddenly so still—because the tug was already too far away or had moored, because no orders, or only muffled ones, were heard—so quiet that one could hear the tinkling or bleating of a herd on the fragrant hill; and one could do nothing but stare dumbstruck at the light everywhere, the small jetty where there were still a few electric bulbs burning, the water without a ripple, a light that spanned all colors from golden red toward the bow to star-filled blue-black above the poop deck, as overwhelming as the scent that one drunkenly inhaled in a speechless admiration that retained nothing of any emotion, any feeling, but was on the contrary an absence, a sense of being relieved of all feeling.

The triangle of Spain—Brabant—Greece. More precisely: Barcelona—Brussels—Rhodes. Should one regret what was initially certainly extreme eccentricity? But if Avignon has now been registered, surrounded, it still hasn't really been singled out—any more than Dijon, Rome, Lyon, Marseille, or Geneva. That will come later. So if his life—coincidence and life are interchangeable—has imposed on him and hence on us this circuitous, interminable approach, why should we try to be brief? Without years of political maneuvering and strategy, there can be no successful siege and thus no joyous entry. No annexation without equipage, reconnaissance, campaigning, laying siege, and storming or negotiating. *The royal army halted before Avignon: its citizens first protested themselves the King's obedient servants, and then refused to grant the army free passage. On June 10th the King, "to avenge the insult done to Christ's army," took an oath that he would not budge till the town was taken, and had his siege-engines set up. After the first panic had subsided, Avignon decided to hold out. Besides, she was a city of the Empire, and had no intention of allowing a King of France to lay down the law for her benefit. The walls were thick, with a strong mercenary garrison and a large citizen-militia to defend them. In fact Avignon fought back with such vigour that for two months the outcome of the war hung in the balance. The King's troops were exposed, not only to hunger, epidemics, and the arrows and quarrels of the besieged, but also to attacks by the forces of the Count of Toulouse, who harried and raided their rear. But while this was going on the King was receiving deputations from various seigneurs and towns in the Midi, who had been impelled to submission both by the presence of the Crusaders and the fear of fresh massacres.* A town is won; one wins someone over. It says in the Bible: "I am a wall, and my breasts are like towers." No wedding night without scouting, spying, approaches, introductions, agreements, contracts. No fertilization—*une femme enceinte, l'enceinte d'une ville*—without spermatozoa squirming upstream for hours, fighting the current and the ravenous appetite of white blood cells, in the face of acidity and heat. Seven circuits of the Kaaba, thirteen circuits of the walls of Jericho. Also the fact that the Comtat Venaissin, of which Avignon became the capital, after Carpentras, remained an imperial territory, surrounded on all sides by French provinces, until 1791, must be significant—certainly for Avignon. It doesn't happen so often that life gives us the opportunity to come into contact with objects, plants, animals, or towns in a way that accords with their own nature. Perhaps it was decreed by fate that he should approach this town as gradually and lengthily and circuitously as its location and history and character demand. Perhaps his experience is limited to that approach? Even then, it is not to be neglected. Approaching may be our most profound vocation. Perhaps we do nothing else in our lifetimes but hedge round, surround things and people with greater or lesser precision, more or less conscientiously, swerving or brushing past them, at most grasping them for a moment, never arriving anywhere for good, except, at the very last, in the earth.

He no longer remembers what led him, in the year of his escape from the "asylum," to begin his hiking trip so far north, in Valence, 120 kilometers from Avignon—or maybe in Montélimar, 80 kilometers away? Perhaps his journey had actually been planned that way, and his ticket obliged him to leave the train that early on; or perhaps the landscape he could see from the compartment window just seemed too southern for him to remain on the train. His knapsack felt heavy as he walked through a grove of plane trees planted on the steep left bank of the Rhone, where elderly men were playing pétanque in the July shade. He hurried through the busy square that was definitely called *Place Clémenceau* or *Place de la République*, feeling

uncomfortable because of his clothes, his knapsack, his solitude—but was it not his own ironic city-dweller's eyes, which
had gazed at the Danes, English, or Dutch wandering through
the center of his hometown, that now, as though reflected back
at him, drove him out of this little town? Then, in the quiet up-
per town, he followed a long, straight, empty street; it was around
midday, the sun erased every trace of life and every shadow, and
he resented the fact that he was finding all this walking difficult,
it was ridiculously early to be tired, and resented how long it was
taking to get out of town, and then he heard girls' voices singing;
he had only to push open a small door, he let his knapsack slide
to the floor and sat down in a pew; it was a dark, cool, almost
chilly space that had room for only ten or so chairs and was
closed off by a gate; beyond, at right angles to this public tran-
sept, was an altar, and on the left in the space in front of it, the
girls, boarding-school students who would soon be going on
holiday, or perhaps orphans, or nuns whose voices had remained
girlish; it was good to sit there, despite the eerie feeling that he
was being observed by invisible eyes from behind the gate; the
ethereal singing that emerged from this cellarlike space and
faded like an icicle melting in the sun was connected to the space
he was soon to enter, was as gratuitously lost, as frankly absurd
as the journey he was now embarked upon. (And if he is asked
now what any of this has to do with Avignon, he'll look at you
with wide, indifferent eyes: "Well, that was just like the beginning of the last encirclement of Avignon, wasn't it?") The first
night—was it in La Bégude-de-Mazenc?—he was given shelter

by an old farmer, whom he'd asked whether the water flowing out of a pipe by the road was drinkable. But the desperate, servile courtesy with which he felt obliged to repay that hospitality, and the discovery, more oppressive than any town walls, of all the human misery a human dwelling can contain—the deaf, disabled farmer's wife, the mentally defective, mumbling and sniggering son or farmhand in whose presence the farmer said that it would have been better if he'd never been born—made him avoid any opportunity for such lodgings from then on. In the evening, after the last village where he had stocked up on provisions, he looked for a quiet, sheltered spot where he could lie down; in the morning his sleeping bag was covered in dew. What had he expected? The evening when he came through Dieulefit, boys and girls were having a running battle on both sides of the main street and he, whichever pavement he may have favored, was essentially forced to walk right down the middle of the street, a rambling northerner. Outcast? by their reciprocal sense of community, inaccessible to him? by their smiles that could just as well have been purely benevolent? He turned his back on them, walking into the evening toward the *Colle du Serre*: Did he perhaps expect that they would send a very young, very pretty girl after him, "Oh stranger, stay with us?" It was nevertheless not just dutiful interest that led him to visit what monuments were along the way. The Merovingian church and the Roman excavations in Vaison, the tower with probably the earliest-known profane frescos in Pernes-les-Fontaines, the inaccessible *Chapelle du Groseau,* built by an Avignon pope, the castle tower at Gordes: these were the places where he could rest without attracting attention, where he had no need to do anything but look, let the light of the objects penetrate his eyes. It was a nuisance, though, that he often had to follow motorways, the cars roaring past made his solitude, his slowness, and his exhaustion feel ridiculous, or at least absurdly artificial—and it wasn't even possible to ignore them, since he had to give way to them with caution. Consequently, it was at a bus stop that he gave in to temptation, after walking for several hours across the plain of Cavaillon: Every patch of ground was under cultivation, the houses were as close together as in Flanders, he certainly wouldn't find a deserted spot to spend the night, or if he did he would be suspected of being a burglar or vagrant, and the tall, dense rows of cypresses that protected the orchards and vineyards from the mistral wind cut off any scenic views anyway. But the day before there had been the trip from Fontaine de Vaucluse to Sénanque via the *Mur de la Peste*, along a path so difficult to see that one had to follow the markers on the tree trunks: The whole of that day he hadn't met a soul except for the shepherd on the top of the plateau who had drawn water for him, he was so thirsty he had knelt down and drunk straight from the bucket; this was quite a different meeting than that with the boys and girls of Dieulefit: they approached each other in a strangely naked, innocent way, the shepherd and he, his thirst was quenched, he was told the time and how far he had to walk, the shepherd was glad to have someone to talk to, his departure was as natural, as unthinking as the sinking of the sun. And yet, the fact that he gave up in Cavaillon, didn't go on to Saint-Rémy and Les Baux (but how out of place and incongruous he would have felt in front of the shops selling pseudo-rustic knickknacks, in front of the rustic three-star hotel, a converted sheepfold for the stinking rich!), gave in to the temptation of a room with a bed in the hotel opposite the station, this fact is not sufficient to explain the uneasiness with which he remembers that trip. The calculation that in the space of a single week, alone, he has covered between 25 and 30 kilometers a day and spent only two nights under a roof, must be enough to satisfy his sporting pretensions. Looking back, it turns out to be extremely disappointing, finding that an exodus from the familiar space and routine of boarding school and parental home and then all his days of receptivity to any new experience whatsoever were not sufficient to involve him in any kind of adventure. What kind of adventure? The kind a twenty-year-old still cares about. Nothing would be better suited to closing the book on the past and yet nothing could be as unadventurous as a commercial traveler's hotel near the train station of a vegetable-trade town. He lacks any experiences of the sort you can hold on to. But wasn't it an experience to look up at the multicolored radiance of the sky in the morning? Certainly everything seems to point to the fact that this was not an experience for him, that he would not be any different now if he hadn't experienced those mornings. He can look now at the postcard he sent from Nyons, *Les Arcades de la Place du Docteur Roux*, and think and say: "I was there then, I think I even bought bread in one of the shops under the gallery when I was there, just like in the picture, everything was dominated by the contrast between the merciless sunlight on the graveled square and the shade under the gallery, a strange shade that was illuminated only *from below*, by the sun reflected off the square"; but, still it is significant that, when five years later his wife bought a skirt in a shop in this same square, he recognized the town only by deductive reasoning and a glance at the map: so was it worthwhile to have stopped off at this place, as slowly as only a pedestrian can? When he looks at the post-card now, it's not principally of his earlier presence in that place that he thinks, but of the possibility of one day staying there—for good? as another person?; living in a couple of rooms above the gallery with a very young, unknown woman, big on sexual experimentation; or alone, doing nothing but abandoning himself to southern torpor. Perhaps in evoking this resentment, he should take account of the exhaustion, of all the various inconveniences that for a city-dweller and a student constitute a "hard life"; one morning while he was washing he discovered that he had stepped on his glasses, and for a day he had to squint and look at other people as little as possible so as not to alarm them with his peculiar gaze; and the morning before his arrival in Cavaillon he happened to notice that one of his soles had turned into a single huge blister, but only afterwards did the pain make it difficult for him to walk. But in his memory the difficulty is not so dominant that it takes the shine off the exceptional, weird nature of the trip. Perhaps the underlying error was that he had ignored or underestimated the anachronistic nature of any hiking trip, anachronistic outside the confines of his person, when cars roared past him, but also within, for example, when in a small town he couldn't resist the temptation to buy a newspaper: real vagrants couldn't read, or didn't read, or made do with old pages left behind by the townsfolk, crumpled up, smeared, and torn. The evening when he reached the gate of the abbey of Sénanque, he was received gruffly by a black-habited, non-Cistercian gatekeeper who gave him nothing but a jug of water and permission to sleep in a wet field; there he heard the voices of students who *were* privileged to enjoy monastic hospitality because they were on a retreat; the next day, after visiting the abbey—church, dormitory, chapter house, and scriptorium—he was annoyed. So what had he expected? Had he really thought that a solitary hiking trip was possible without waging a dogged, arrogant rebellion against the inhabited, everyday world? Yes, the anachronism was mainly in himself, an inability to live up to the reality offered him, to enter unvarnished reality in an uninhibited way. A student is as little capable of being a temporary vagrant as a vagrant is of being a temporary student. Cars roaring past only bother a pedestrian who doesn't consider himself completely redundant. An adventure can only befall someone who doesn't expect or desire one. Only a person who has reached the point of wanting no other happiness and perhaps no happiness at all can draw happiness from a sun-drenched square, from waking up under an open sky. Anyone wanting to see a reality—a dawn, a woman, a fruit, a town—must also tune both his imagination and his senses to reality. "What has that trip got to do with Avignon?" Perhaps his thorough dissatisfaction was necessary for him to return there, for him to try a different way of appropriating this country. And then he traces his route on a map: it shows a surprising symmetry with the Rhone, the turning-point in Pernes corresponds to the bend in the river at Sorgues, that in Hordes to the bend at Vallabrègues, and Cavaillon to Tarascon: the town of Avignon lies between the river and the route followed then like a walnut between the as yet unclosed arms of a nutcracker.

(Where is this report heading? Shouldn't Avignon be more than a pretext for a concatenation of more or less relevant anecdotes? But: can an object be grasped by us other than in a slimy mass of events, experiences, memories? The thing is to learn how to approach a reality, any reality. It isn't true that the reality of books is more beautiful than that of life, it's precisely the other way round, the reality of life is incomparably more beautiful than that of books, and not for some aesthetic, moral, or philosophical reason: quite simply *by definition. Is it possible, this nothing thinks, that one has not yet seen, recognized, and said anything real and important? Is it possible that one has had thousands of years of time to look, reflect, and write down, and that one has let the millennia pass away like a school recess in which one eats one's sandwich and an apple?—Yes, it is possible.—Is it possible that in spite of inventions and progress, in spite of culture, religion, and worldly wisdom, that one has remained on the surface of life? Is it possible that one has even covered this surface, which would at least have been something, with an incredibly dull slipcover, so that it looks like living-room furniture during the summer vacation?—Yes, it is possible,* thinks a Dane in his fifth-floor Paris apartment. It's possible that every supposedly objectifying model is nothing more than a fraud, doing nothing to correct our faulty vision, but giving us the illusion that our eyes have been opened. How could our verbal victory over the opacity and discontinuity and dullness of life not be illusory, when we ourselves prefer the modalities of its fragmentation and lack of transparency? So, is this all only for the sake of life, instead of art for the sake of an art disguised as life? Is art no longer anything but the servant of life? As if art had ever been dependent on our lives. But writing is no longer a self-satisfied game providing us a reassuring or enchanting optical illusion. A representation then? But how are words supposed to be a faithful representation of, for example, a delicate, long- and straight-haired girl sitting on a sunny step in tight jeans and a sweater with her still ripening breasts beneath it, looking at and timidly eyed by a young man? of a trip that consisted of two hundred thousand steps, of some five hundred thousand usually mostly empty seconds? "Disillusion" or "anachronism" are no more than crude shorthand, extremely colorful symptoms of a diffuse malaise—not so much of representation, hopeless in advance, but of any dogged and likewise hopeless word-by-word approach to a reality. Limitation of writing? Only writing occupies the whole space through which life at its most abundant can be approached; there is no integral approach to life that does not partake of writing. But it can only ever be of any use to us when we focus our *knowing* gaze—that divine gaze in which we can only hope with unreasonable obstinacy we will one day partake—on a life actually lived. It is inevitable that he who thinks this abandons all fictional translation, all those astonishingly vain literary forms, presentations, distortions. Invented stories, morality, psychology, symbolism, structure—all laughably unreliable, henceforth. But, then, those contrivances that turn out, in retrospect, to be a gift from life—fate, coincidence, providence—or from reality—a trip, a girl, a town—can be all the more eagerly accepted.)

He returned to this land of olives and cypresses, lavender and thyme, but this time *differently*. The following summer he spent five weeks in a village not far from Vachères, in the hills east of Avignon, and didn't do much more than walk through and around the village for hours on end until he got to know the place almost better than the natives. Above the village, adjacent to the ruined *prieuré*, with, in the remains of a garden, those two tall, dead straight cypresses visible for miles around, was the unused Romanesque *haute église*, with, in front of its porch, an old lime tree and a bench from where one could look down upon the blunted roofs and the provincial road that climbed up to the village. Down below in the square with the fountain and the traditional restaurant was the Renaissance *basse église*—and between the two churches one saw almost nothing but piles of rubble, as if the village had slid slowly down the hill, and was still sliding, since the *Place du Tertre* with the *mairie* and the *bar-tabac* outside where the Digne-Marseille bus stopped twice a day was still further downhill, so that the *basse église* was becoming a second *haute église*. There was a promenade sheltered from the mistral running from the *Place du Tertre* to the *lavoir*; past the municipal school ran a country road onto which the back doors to the gardens of the houses on the main street opened. Outside the village there was a Romanesque *Chapelle Saint-Jean* on a hilltop, and a Romanesque *Chapelle Saint-Paul* in a valley; there was an eighteenth-century chateau with a pond, and a nineteenth-century chateau with a densely planted park and a terrace surrounded by a stone balustrade from which one could look down at the *nationale cent* that runs from Avignon to Digne; and scattered everywhere were large, separate, often abandoned farms: *La Fontyon, La Calade, La Saint-Sébastien, Le Lavandon, Saint-Babylas, Le Trigaden, La Bénédicte*. So was that the way to get to know a stretch of countryside? Once, in a late afternoon, he was walking around lost in the tall undergrowth at the foot of a hill, and when he had walked completely round it he suddenly came face to face with the village, whose houses, colored ochre by the late sun, lay as if piled up against the next hill: this was a recognition of what had obviously become *his* village, as moving as a long hoped-for homecoming. So why was there still unease, embarrassment, and lack of fulfillment? Suddenly people turned out to be incomparably more difficult to approach than stones. Not the old Avignon widow Rose Escoffier in whose house on the *Place du Tertre* he was staying; in the mornings she remained invisible, anyone who saw her in the afternoon realized that she needed a whole morning to do up and powder her face the way she did, and besides, he took his three daily meals in the restaurant; apart from that she had to look after her deaf, invalid mother, who was so ancient that despite her cheerful nature he could never manage to spend more than a few minutes with her, as if he were afraid that such great age was contagious. But there was the boy at whose lithe body—dark, slanted eyes; dazzling teeth; slim, taut thighs—he stole jealously fascinated glances, pretending to watch the game of pétanque. And there was his table companion in the village restaurant, the tall, no longer very young woman from Strasbourg, with whom he was so excessively embarrassed that it was several days before he was able to eat around her, as though she were some Messalina eager to rape him—but his shyness did not allow such a thought even to arise, and when she told him about the quiet spot where she spent her afternoons sunning herself, it never occurred to him that this might be an invitation. But above all there was Danièle—how wrong that sentence is. Initially there was only a nameless, burgeoning girl of about fourteen, with long, straight, dark-blonde hair whom he'd first noticed among her girlfriends during a Provençale Mass in the *haute église*, because she looked up at him so often. It was the same delicate girl he bumped into some days later, in the street, among her girlfriends, adorned with a brightly colored necklace and jangling bracelets, wearing lipstick; maybe he wouldn't have been sure it was her if she hadn't looked at him so compellingly, as her girlfriends giggled—only later was it to occur to him that this formidable giggling that had so undermined him might also have been directed at her. She was the girl who almost every afternoon as he was dining came to draw water from the fountain in front of the restaurant, and in the evening during supper passed by with a clanking milk can; there was always an opportunity for her to cast a glance into the bar, even though the bead curtain was closed—she jerked her head to the right or to the left, her look never seeming anything more than the result of this gesture, which caused her long, loose hair to sweep over her shoulder. It was the same girl who once stopped next to him during a Sunday Mass, at the back of the church, although her girlfriends were beckoning to her from the front, and he allowed himself just one timid look at her wide, pink dress. One can say all this now, simply, clearly, and no one will refuse to see in her actions strangely bold advances; indeed, *at the time* it was perfectly clear even to strangers: One afternoon when he was dining outside with a couple he had made friends with, the wife, who was sitting opposite him facing the square, observed with a smile: "Oh, the looks she's giving you!"—the girl was standing by the fountain and staring at his back. Why was it that he didn't notice it at the time, that he couldn't see, or didn't want to see, or refused to admit to himself what he saw? Or: How was it possible for him to remain *insincerely* arrogantly unapproachable? Once when she strolled towards him, picking berries with her girlfriends while he was sitting reading under the lime tree in front of the *haute église*, his inertia in the face of her movements, which *might have been* advances (since he was to have certainty only later, too late, when his contemptible character no longer seemed so self-evident), his inertia seemed so shameful to him that, just as the girls were about to leave again, hesitantly, he was on the point of giving in and speaking. What kind of fool was he to ignore this trembling longing while the tongues of his desire licked every part of her body? Sometimes he thought: "If I can speak to her alone, I'll do it." He did not know how to behave other than as a cowardly, vulgar seducer. The shrill laughter of girls is a formidable obstacle for someone who feels nothing but shame about sex. But the fact that right at the end he did dare to ask her two friends in the street where "la troisième" had got to—and then he heard her name for the first time—proves that he did not fear her friends as intensely as she herself. (And his trembling smile then was certainly no different from the old gentlemen in municipal parks vainly offering sweets to pitiless, forewarned children.) The friends said that she had gone to a nearby town. Gone, not returned—so would he see her again after all? For a long time she remained invisible. Why didn't he realize at the time that the shame he felt was being set aside, stockpiled, until it became an inexhaustible store? This regret, years later, would well up in his throat and make him groan, so that the day would finally come when he would give anything—not finally to press her frantically against the hard, prickly earth, since bottled up desire can never be retrieved—but to apologize for being such a fool, a bastard, an indecent idiot: "Pardonne-moi, je suis un pauvre con." Certainly, he knew nothing. He knew nothing?

The distorting, impure things he knew all too well. He knew very well, as if instinctively, how to go about getting into Madame Escoffier's good graces, so that, for instance, his smile should never appear excessive to her, and he knew likewise that he must believe her when she maintained that *cours d'amour* were once held on her tenanted farm *Les Craux*; true, it was a little more difficult when he heard her screaming at her mother to believe that she wasn't just tormenting the old woman, but was only trying to penetrate her deafness by force; though it was easy enough, when she gave him her poems to read, which she had written once under the name of "Rose de Provence" (*L'arôme capiteux des roses* / *Pénètre l'ombre du boudoir* / *Et le frisson ailé du soir* / *Effleure nos paupières closes*) to encourage her to confuse his amazement with admiration. From where did he derive the knowledge that he had only to treat her as an unsuspected Anna de Noailles to be seen as a charming guest? He received his reward—when Madame Escoffier returned to Avignon, he was allowed to stay on in her house alone. What good was a house that he would have to leave tomorrow, when he would never again see the girl who'd had to go to the next town? But she was sitting on the step of her parents' rented house, her delicate body jammed into her jeans and tight-fitting sweater, impossible to talk to because two boys were already standing there talking to her, and he thought he heard one of the boys ask: "C'est lui?" It got dark, but however tiring the next day's journey might be, this was no time to sleep; the fact that she had returned from town the day before his departure was far too miraculous, it must mean that he was being given a last chance. While he dithered around the *haute église*, he heard a woman's voice calling down: "Danièle! Dany!," probably for supper—but where had she suddenly got to? Off with one of the boys perhaps? He went on stumbling through pitch-black alleyways for a long time, and then decided he might as well pack his case and go to bed—in despair, finally, and trying to smother his yearning in grim contempt for the girl who'd sat on her front step like a whore (yet only much later was he to think of the possibility that she had left the step with the *two* boys). But he didn't get away as lightly as that. Just as he was about to get undressed he heard through his open window (through which, for the last few evenings, the clunk of pétanque balls had no longer been sounding) girls' voices below, talking under the lime trees in front of the *mairie*. Then he took a chance, after some dizzying minutes of hesitation, on doing what he should have done four weeks before: He went down the stairs of Madame Escoffier's house and struck up a conversation with the girls. What he said at the time isn't important, the backlog could no longer be bridged with words; and the fact that Danièle remained surprisingly silent can be explained in all kinds of ways. For now it was better to let her peeping, sniggering, garrulous girlfriends go on chattering—only the most brilliant of gestures might still have been able to restore the desire that had been spurned. *A lover is always timorous. One trembles at the unexpected sight of the beloved. Every lover grows pale at the sight of the beloved.* How different from him those *fervestus* must have been, on whom the *règles d'Amour* had to be imposed as novel, sometimes laughably far-fetched rules of the game. How awkward, how clumsy his body felt. So much so that it may have been he who said good-bye. Perhaps it was enough for him to have heard that Danièle lived in Orange? She was the only one who waved after him: "A Noël!" And instead of running after her, taking her by the hand away from her friends and dragging her with him in a mad flight through the darkness to some corner where no one would find them, where triumphant, rejuvenating words would be panted and stammered, he went to bed, dazed, numbed, dumbstruck . . . Such things happen. Meaning: it happens that we don't give the most natural things the chance or the space to occur. One should beware of attributing such pathetic deficiencies to life. We are the guilty ones, and our predecessors—everyone. Sometimes we don't have a clue about the most elementary rules of the game—that we really do have to want to win, for one; that, by and large, and all things considered, we should all be living for our own pleasure—and so, if others omit to teach us these rules, we sometimes come to regard it as a duty, indeed something commendable, to lose. And love? Love is never born out of self-torment, but out of a need for full enjoyment . . . But he's not yet ready for that knowledge, as a blue bus takes him along the valley of the Coulon and the Durance to Avignon. He doesn't even think: "Now I've succeeded in adapting to a country, hills, plants, and stones, but it turns out that—just as in Dieulefit—I'm still incapable of relating to my fellow human beings, treating them in a humane and uninhibited way." Either he has misunderstood all Danièle's gestures and made a fool of himself by his indecision and his ultimate approach, or his girls are not only approachable, but *long* to be approached, and then his desires, smothered in shame, must be acknowledged as natural longings (the fugitive who presses himself against a door as if the wood could swallow him up now feels the door give way: Will he truly be able to step into the unknown room that he had already abandoned all hope of entering?). In his astonishment he *sits* amid a din that paralyses all his senses. In Paris he will spend the night in the room of a young whore decorated with dolls and velvet animals—for although he may dimly suspect that certain girls might come to tolerate his desires, for the moment all he knows for certain is that this whore is willing to do so immediately, for money; he won't question her about her behavior, and only years later will he admit how unforgettably friendly she was. In Brussels he will receive a few letters from Madame Escoffier: "Que ne puis-je, pour chasser vos brumes, glisser dans cette envelope un brin du léger mistral qui souffle, un coin de ciel bleu, et un beau rayon de soleil," and reply at least once, until he finally realizes how utterly pathetic this misplaced flirting is. But he will not yet awaken from his lethargic bewilderment.

Notice that Orange has been mentioned, so that now only the names of Tarascon or Saint-Rémy need to be included for Avignon to be nominally enclosed, geographically circumscribed. But here difficulties arise. Because he remembers next to nothing specific about the next ten passing visits to Avignon. People live in such a casual way that they can stop off in a town and go on living as if this had never happened, or else only happened once, in circumstances as vague and contradictory as a dream. And yet, the English squire whose *Diary* can be found in his library suspected, when he entered Avignon on October 3, 1644, that he would never return, and it may be thanks to this realization on the part of a conscious mortal (*partir c'est mourir un peu*: in the place that we will never visit again, we experience something of our death) that later, in Sayes Court, Deptford, he was able to write: *Hence leaving our barque, we tooke horse (seing but at some distance the Towne & Principality of Orange; and lodging one night on the Way arrived by noone at Avignon: This Citty has belong'd to the Popes ever since Clem: the 6ts tyme, being Anno 1352, alienated by Jeane, Queen of Naples and Sicily. Entring the gates, the soldiers at the guard took our Pistols and Carbines from us, and examin'd us very strictly; after that, having obtain'd the Governors leave & Vice-Legat to tarry 3 dayes, we were civily conducted to our lodging.* We are usually so badly informed about reality. So will those passing visits of his simply remain unmentioned? But that would mean to neglect the sediment undoubtedly formed by those arrivals, thereby falsifying his later view of Avignon. Shall we confine ourselves to that sediment, by for example shuffling together all those defectively remembered visits in passing, amalgamating them into a single, now satisfactory, integrated sort of visit in passing? This is how a common variety of literature works, condensing a campaign into a single battle, boiling down all the gestures and actions of courtship into a single, orgiastic advent; it looks for what we *want* to see in reality, unthinkingly transcribing the myth evoked in us by reality—not what is offered us, modestly, even fundamentally, in that reality. However, it would be no less a falsification to respect the fragmentary succession of those passing visits, but to make them more worth writing or reading about by padding them out with imagination. What do we know about the postulates, the basic rules of remaining faithful to life? We write *afternoon* instead of *early evening*, *Geneva* instead of *Prague*; one omits to betray an uncertainty, one misses a *perhaps,* a *who knows*, a question mark—and immediately we have lost an opportunity, have forfeited something, we don't know what, reaching God knows how far into our lives, something that should have been given us by objects, phenomena, facts, events. So there is nothing for it but to accept the fragmentation and the superficiality and the emptiness, and with each journey to restrict oneself as precisely as possible to what can be written, faithfully, about reality.

One. A winter train journey southward to Avignon via Paris, and then the blue bus to nearby the village. The three kilometers between the *nationale cent* highway down in the valley and the village have to be covered on foot, or else you have to ring the *bar-tabac* from Paris or Avignon so that the landlord can drive his car out to where the main road begins; for some unknown reason, or just so as he can charge more, he's perfectly happy to drive eight kilometers to meet the bus on the *nationale cent*; thus, after his first few trips there, the traveler decided it was simpler and cheaper to walk the provincial road, even though that means arriving sweaty and out of breath in the village from the constant climbing. He stays in the restaurant. The girl Danièle who called "A Noël" after him, who in Brussels has become more powerfully absent with every passing month and week, in Paris and Avignon with every passing hour, doesn't appear in the village, the only place where he might reasonably expect her presence. When he suspects that he will not be able to see her again, he will have an overwhelming sense of what he neglected in her, and has now irrevocably forfeited. Later, perhaps because it's impossible to live with such regret, events will start to blur, becoming as questionable as the memory of a dream.

Two. By bus to Avignon, by train to Paris. "Returning from Avignon I got to Paris *Gare du Nord* at about eight in the evening. There was no train to Brussels indicated, so I took my suitcase to the baggage check office, went for a coffee in a bistro, and strolled as far as Pigalle. But it was Saturday and there was a fair—one tent promised *Tableaux vivants et danses lascives*—and I prefer the *Hôtel Biron* to the bustle of the boulevards. I did, though, stay for a glass of wine in a bar, because there was a whore who looked at me just like Danièle did, and she had the same eyes and the same mouth; but now it was winter, and she went upstairs with a customer. So I went back to the station, intending to spend the night in the waiting room.

"The station was closed. A cold drizzle was falling. A tramp was sleeping on the ground in front of one of the closed doors. A large, brightly lit café attracted me: *Ouvert jour et nuit*. A young guy with an eye patch sat staring into his beer glass. A trio of young men with a girl—like a slender thoroughbred, I thought—were operating the jukebox. I ordered a beer, and lit up a Gitane. A tramp came in with a woman, old and with a masculine face; the tramp executed a few dance steps to the music. I asked the waiter when the station opened: 'At four-thirty.' I looked at my watch: one-thirty. The waiter walked up and down, but my glass wasn't empty yet. The tramp looked at me for a long time in silence; I could feel his eyes. A bitter taste of vomit in my throat. I went to the toilet, paid, and left.

"I didn't know where I was going. I found a closed café, with the chairs outside under the awning. I sat down. Another Gitane, and the same acid taste in my throat. Sometimes the wind gusted down the empty street; the tables were damp from the rain. I put up my collar, a cold strip along the nape of my neck. A few people came by and went into a hotel. A drunk came staggering along. Saw me and turned back. Suddenly I felt like mussels. Somewhere I'd read: 'Moules marinières.' I wanted to eat mussels, raw, with vinaigrette sauce and white bread. I stood up, I was cold and set out to look for a better refuge. A man was sleeping on his feet. Resting his head on the roof of a car.

"Under a large canvas with wind flaps a tramp was sleeping on the ground, against a suitcase, with his head leaning on a chair. I sat down beside him and thought of raw mussels. Then we were joined by two men; the first may have been a Corsican, still young, short, slight build, with a thin moustache; the other broad-chested, strong, with a flat nose. The latter asked if I had any money for a room; I said it wasn't worth it now. For a moment I was going to admit that I was just doing this on a whim, but caught myself just in time. He started sounding off about young people nowadays who spent the night on deserted café terraces. The other man smiled bashfully. A woman came out of the café, perhaps the owner's wife, she pushed the chair away from under the tramp and he fell heavily and flatly to the ground.

"I said to the flat-nosed one that I wanted to eat some mussels. He replied that in that case I should go to the *Jour et nuit*. I thought that was friendly of him. But he got agitated and furious: So was I going for mussels or not? And I had to leave right away. He grabbed me by the collar. I slunk off, not even humiliated, just flabbergasted. Even now I don't understand.

"I went into the café again. The guy with the bandaged eye was still sitting there, talking to some soldiers. At a table further on sat a young man with a very gloomy and exhausted look. In a distant corner a couple were necking. To my left was a fat woman, still young, with long, dark straight hair, light sandals, and light-blue slacks. A little further on two young guys, asleep, elbows on the table; then an old gentleman absorbed in a newspaper. I ordered a plate of 'moules marinières' with a glass of white wine. The fat woman occasionally turned to me; I pretended not to see her. A gang of young people came in, talking and laughing loudly, back from a dance. The waiter brought the mussels, which were a disappointment: I didn't know that 'moules marinières' were cooked mussels; but the sauce was good.

"A couple came in, the woman young, slim, and beautiful, possibly a model, the man nondescript and in love. They sat down two tables ahead of me, with their backs to the fat woman. The man whispered sweet nothings into the ear of his model, she looked at me—the man couldn't see—and kissed him. The fat woman turned to me and asked if the mussels were good; I said they were, but didn't offer her any. The young partygoers left, as did the courting couple after a while. The fat woman giggled to herself. A man offered some of his drink, but she refused. I ordered a cup of coffee.

"The waiter came and pushed the table away from under the sleepers: It was time they ordered something. The owner came along. I was afraid the old gentleman was asleep behind his newspaper. The fat woman was talking to a cat, but was looking furtively at the waiter, afraid. I paid and left.

"Three whores were standing talking under a tarpaulin. I offered them a Gitane. The oldest one wanted to take me with her, she was fat, faded, short. It's dreadful, someone trying to make you want them when one feels nothing but revulsion for them. We talked a bit, about the oldest one's new umbrella, about the movie they were going to see the next day. Perhaps they didn't trust me, because they split up.

"I stayed by myself and sat down in a corner on a round table. It was raining, and the rain was splashing down off the tarpaulin. A handsome black guy passed, tall, slim, in a white raincoat. I felt rotten. A Gitane caused the same acrid taste in my mouth. Then I began whispering Baudelaire. I retrieved the words laboriously: 'Et comme un long sanglot . . . Et comme un long sanglot . . . Et comme un long linceul traînant à l'orient . . .' The fat young woman in blue slacks walked past, perhaps chased off by the waiter. A man crept out of a corner somewhere and tried to buttonhole her, but she went on walking. The fat whore also went past, a disgustingly short coquettish monster under an umbrella. She said it was bad weather, and that such weather shouldn't be visited upon poor people.

"The station opened up. The waiting room was full of down-and-outs who had spent the night there, it smelled of breath and armpit sweat. I found an empty seat and almost jumped out of my skin: On the front page of a newspaper was a photo of Danièle. I read the caption: It was only Danièle showing off her new hairstyle. Then I fell asleep."

Three. One spring, together with a friend, south to Avignon, west from Avignon. Now, eight years later, one can consult a railway timetable—the times can't have changed that much. The blue bus left Avignon at about six-thirty, morning and night—but he never or only very occasionally took the night bus because then he would only reach the fork in the valley at about nine in the evening and only get to the village at about ten. So the train that is now called FR and left the *Gare de Lyon* at eleven in the evening didn't reach Avignon until six-thirty-six the following day? Maybe just in time to catch the bus (because the bus was only occasionally right on time), but theoretically not. Other possibilities are: the twenty-one train at three minutes to eight in the evening from the *Gare de Lyon*, arriving at Dijon at eight minutes to eleven, ten to three in Lyon, five-fifteen in Avignon; train nineteen, *Paris-Côte d'Azur* at eight P.M. from the *Gare de Lyon*, eight minutes to eleven in Dijon, twelve minutes to one in Lyon, four minutes past three in Avignon; train sixty-one at fourteen minutes to ten in the evening from the *Gare de Lyon*, thirteen minutes to one in Dijon, ten to three in Lyon, five-fifteen in Avignon. After a few journeys it became clear that even when it wasn't compulsory, as with the *Mistral*, he needed to book a seat if he didn't want to spend the whole journey from Paris to Avignon standing in the corridor: The SNCF apparently only provided as many carriages as were necessary to accommodate the seats reserved, and anyone without a reservation could only hope that he'd get to the station early enough to find a carriage that wasn't completely sold out. *Le train soixante et un à destination de: Dijon—Lyon—Avignon—Marseille—Nice—Menton—Vintimille, départ vingt et une heure quarante-six, voie cinq, les voyageurs en voiture s'il vous plaît—Dis-lui bien que Marcel ne pourra pas venir avant—Non, laisse, cela n'a plus d'importance—Nicole! c'est ici, Nicole—Mais monsieur quand je vous dis que cette place—Au revoir, n'oublie pas de lui dire—Hé Brichaud vise la poupée—Non laisse, laisse—Jacquot reste ici—Au revoir, au revoir.*

Four. On the return journey it was difficult or impossible to book a seat, the Brussels travel agencies refused to arrange it, and in order to do it on the way out from Paris or Avignon you had to know in advance the exact day and time of your return journey, which seemed an unpleasant restriction of one's freedom. The bus to Avignon passed the junction of the *route nationale* and the provincial road at a quarter to eight in the morning and a quarter past five in the evening, and stopped if one signaled. There was a way of covering the stretch as far as the *route nationale* on foot without hiring a taxi: You could continue some distance on the Marseille bus, which stopped at the village and in about eight kilometers followed the same *nationale cent* as the Avignon bus, the only problem being that you had to wait for between half an hour and three-quarters of an hour for the blue bus to show. You arrived in Avignon at a quarter to ten in the morning or a quarter to eight in the evening; if the former, you could catch the ten-thirty-three train or the twelve minutes past one, which arrived in Paris at six minutes past seven or one minute to eight, but offered no connection to Brussels except the very slow night train—obviously only connecting with the Paris-Liège service. (In order to travel on the *Trans-Europe Express* leaving at eighteen minutes to nine, one had to have reserved a seat in advance, or else one had to find a reserved but still unoccupied seat at the last minute.) In the latter case, one caught one of the evening trains—seven minutes to eleven, one minute to eleven, or two minutes to twelve—all of which arrived in

Paris at between a quarter to seven and ten to eight; then there were trains at the *Gare du Nord* at eight minutes to eight or twenty past ten or eight minutes past three in the afternoon or at twenty-six minutes past four. So as a rule the journey took at least about eighteen hours, and not infrequently traffic was slowed down even further by strikes.

Five. One summer, alone. Approaching Avignon from the north meant approaching through the country of the cypress and the olive tree. One tall, perfectly straight and slim, the dense black-green foliage accessible only to small birds, a tree that provides no usable fruits, and not even any shade in the hottest part of the day; which stands perpendicular and for miles around indicates the location of a dwelling or a grave; which becomes useful only, because of its almost indestructible wood, after it has been felled. The other squat, wide, gnarled, the branches seemingly arbitrarily twisted and tortured, the silvery green leaves so thin that at night the stars shine through them and in the afternoon one cannot shelter beneath them; but bringing forth the most abundant fruit. The country where very small flocks of sheep graze on almost nothing on the stony hills except thyme and wild lavender and *poivre d'âne* and juniper bushes—the hunters and the thrushes wait for those too, in the autumn; where the merciless light makes those who leave their cool houses dizzy all at once, and gives them the feeling that their bodies will soon float up into the hot air; where the sun very slowly drives sugar into the grapes and incomprehensibly juicy melons; the country where the winds are so much the opposite of fleeting or capricious that, like rivers, they have been given names: *tramontane, vent du soleil, mistral.*

Six. On his return to the north he is taken to Avignon Station in a car, in the back are two girls, the one called Maria is wearing dark glasses. Are they going to be traveling with him?

"No, once the train has left, they'll drive back to the village."

So why are they coming along?

"Well, in the village he shared the same house with them. In the evenings they would make a big wood fire and listen to him read aloud from *The Notebooks of Malte Laurids Brigge: Those were the days of that Avignon Christianity that a generation before had gathered around John the Twenty-second, with so many involuntary refugees following him that, on the site of his pontificate, the mass of this palace immediately arose, closed in and heavy like an emergency shelter for all the homeless souls."*

All right, but why is Maria wearing dark glasses now?

"Probably she doesn't want people to look at her eyes."

But why on earth not?

"Well, one evening they had all been walking through the dark village with some friends, and in the arched passageway to the promenade he'd yelled something, just to startle the girls, and Maria, trembling, had pressed herself up against him . . ."

And was that all?

"Well, in the evenings they often lay down on the road, on the asphalt, looking up at the falling stars, and he held her hand in his . . ."

And was that all?

"Well, the morning before he left, she came to wake him to watch the sunrise . . ."

And he kissed her?

"Yes, he probably did."

"And is it true that she'll get sick after her return from Avignon?"

"Yes."

And that in a letter, later, she'll call him *the only one I can rely on*?

"Yes."

And that she'll be sorry that she isn't *on his level*, that she can't *manage to write exalted letters* to him?

"Yes."

And that there will come a time when she complains that he no longer writes to her?

"Yes, but . . ."

But what?

"But—nothing."

And that he'll get to the point where he slyly avoids being alone with her?

"Yes. Yes. Yes. Yes. Yes."

Seven. One winter, to the village, which in his mind is increasingly inhabited by various people. People: Madame Escoffier's aloofly smiling sister and her short, thin, pale husband, a retired engineer—one could never tell whether or when he was smiling; the landlord of the *bar-tabac*, a former truck-driver with the sinister face of a boxer; his dark-eyed, gray-haired wife, hailing from the biggest farm in the area, the very picture of solid, sensible, passionate womanhood; the gruff, paunchy *maire* who always spent the whole day playing cards in the *bar-tabac* opposite his house; the old, retired head chef of a grammar school in Algiers and Digne, who since his wife's death—which had caused him to faint dead away—had lived alone with a fat, dirty keeshond dog in a house close to the restaurant where he ate every day; the impressively neat, white-haired, ever-smiling woman who lived next door to the restaurant and about whom he never heard a thing, not even her name; the young, thin landlord, so taciturn and phlegmatic that in the village he was called *le mime*, but beaming with pride at every successful aioli or a mature Banon cheese; his wife, from Limoges, taller than her husband, bright and happy, who described the Banon cheese as "celui qui pue" when she wanted to tease her husband, and everyone in the village wondered how a slob like him had come by such a pretty girl; the good-natured, white-mustached *maire* with whom he had talked quite a bit, and who had died shortly before his third trip to the village; the old man's sister and his wife, the two village gossips in the strategically located corner house right opposite the low church; the vulgar, unreliable woman from Paris with whom two children had been boarded; the thick-set, wheezing priest who did nothing but collect antiques; the giggling grocer who everyone knew was cheating them, and his shrilly chattering wife who when her husband was around was always frightened to death of being too honest; the short, strongly-built baker in *tricot-de-peau* and his red-haired, puffy wife with the medieval-sounding girl's name; and Richaud, the drunk and odd-job man, and his wife who in Flanders would have been called a "floozy"; and the thin-as-a-rake housecleaner and washerwoman dressed in rags who was so astonishingly like Dulle Griet in Brueghel's picture that he could no longer see the character as the symbol of disastrous violence; her pathologically overweight husband who did little else but drink, to whom he had once heard the six-year-old son of the *mime* say "J'ai vu un cochon gros comme toi, et il avait la tête qui te ressemblait"; the bricklayer, oldest in the town, who died of cancer—and who, in his final week, raved horribly at his wife, a woman he ordinarily loved very much; and the skinny sister of the priest and her equally skinny and timid, though underhanded daughter, one of Danièle's friends; and the two brothers who, by the time the eldest died, had lived together on their farm for forty years; and the postman's not yet nubile daughter, who was almost disturbingly beautiful; and the young, ginger-haired primary-school teacher, who along with the *mime* was the only Marxist in the village; and the mother of the *mime* who lived in the *Place du Tertre* and was the only one who went to Mass every single morning; and the still-young carpenter from Marseille who had moved to the privacy of the village with his wife after winning the grand prize in the lottery; and the house painter who called himself Monsieur Georges—perhaps he thought people couldn't tell he was a Jew, but he just couldn't resist the temptation to refer to the Jews in every conversation, whether appropriate or not, calling them "the others"—and who might even have become a great artist if his canvases hadn't been dangerously similar to Dufy's; and then the woman who lived with Monsieur Georges, a Creole or mulatto who was once supposed to have been ravishingly beautiful; and the widow of a member of parliament who may have been executed—she played the harmonium on Sundays and probably lived in proud and appalling poverty; and then the oldest woman in the entire village, who, however, was sent off to an old people's home before she actually reached the age of a hundred, and who once said to him, as she watched the children romping about in front of the church: "Et tous plus beaux les uns que les autres"—and how it appalled him to think that someone could get so old and yet still have exactly the same thoughts as he. "People people people," he thinks, his head spinning ... That they are all alive or have been alive, and that everyone alive will die. That the earth, apart from these words and perhaps a few archives to commemorate them, will one day be again as though they've never lived. That, in fact, the earth at present looks just as it would look if countless such people had never existed. That one can't tell by looking at the village that if all the people who ever lived there suddenly came back, there wouldn't be room to move. Heaven is indispensable: only there can we imagine that there would be room enough.

Eight. The same winter, west as far as Avignon, then north to Paris where he had made a rendezvous at the *Gare du Nord* with the blonde Brussels girl to whom he had sworn eternal friendship. On the morning when he walked down the provincial road to the *route nationale*, he penetrated the fog that still occupied the valley. That made waiting for the blue bus an exciting experience: Would it loom unexpectedly out of the fog and drive blindly by? One could listen closely, but because there was a sharp bend in the *route nationale* just before the turn-off, in order to skirt a ravine, the sound of each approaching vehicle was magnified and echoed and dispersed evenly in the fog, so he just stood close to the road next to his suitcase as though mesmerized, hardly daring to take a few steps up and down, even when it was completely quiet; but on each occasion the driver saw him in time, and in the bus one could come to one's senses again, as in an inhabited house, and as long as there was nothing to be seen out the windows, one could always look at a fellow passenger—a girl, a boy, the occasional woman, dressed to kill.

As far as Cavaillon the bus followed a tributary of the Durance. Anyone needing to get off went and asked the driver to stop, and his departure was always observed by the other passengers; in a village the traveler disappeared into the first café, or down a side street, but sometimes he was met by chattering men and women and his appearance provoked exclamations and expansive gestures; but sometimes it was at a crossroads in some open fields that the bus stopped, and if the person disembarking wasn't met by anyone, it was impossible not to look back at him for as long as possible, walking alone down a side road stretching so far that one often couldn't see where it led. Halfway through the trip, in Apt, there was a stop; not in the town square, but in a smaller one on the far side of town, where the road crosses the river and then turns to follow the right bank; the conductor and the driver went into a café-hotel, and you had time to visit the urinal, to buy a paper or a packet of cigarettes, or drink an espresso. After Apt it was rare for anyone else to get on, and those who did were probably people who had missed the ordinary bus to Cavaillon. It was a very significant valley that the bus traversed for some sixty kilometers. To the right of the road the *plateau de Vaucluse* climbed slowly northward towards the broad, bare, recumbent *Montagne de Lure* and *Mont Ventoux*, ancient, peaceful Alpine foothills, a summer grazing area for the herders and shepherds who pass through when changing from low to high pastures; on the left rose the steep, recalcitrant, darkly wooded northern slope of the Lubéron chain, foothills of the Pyrenees, a haunt for birds of prey and wild boar, once a sanctuary for persecuted Waldensians, the infrequent villages empty or alarmingly dirty, their inhabitants tainted by inbreeding—somewhere there stood the tower from which Gypsies had cursed and bewitched the area, and there too were the ruins of the castle where Louis-Aldonse-Donatien or Donatien-Alphonse-François de Sade had refused, or neglected, to sink into obscurity. Shortly before Coustellet, on the right, almost at the top of the slope, the white buildings of Gordes became visible, and then one leaves the *nationale cent* and turns left, along the edge of the last foothills of the Lubéron, onto the road where he had once interrupted his hiking trip. In Cavaillon the bus stopped in the station square, just in front of the hotel where he had spent the night, then—but it was only after two or three journeys that he realized this. After Cavaillon the bus didn't stop again, driving past orchards and vegetable gardens divided by cypress hedges and irrigation channels, all the way to the foot of the *Chartreuse de Bonpas,* where it turned onto the *nationale sept,* which comes from Aix and crosses the Durance at Noves. From there, immediately after the airfield, Avignon was clearly in evidence: the land less frantically industrially exploited, the farms old and sometimes almost in ruins . . . but noble. As one drove past the new *halles* and the goods station (where the sleeper trains also arrived), travelers who were getting off at the first town gate started standing up. But the bus drove on, as far as the station entrance.

—In Paris he was to sleep with the blonde girl for the first time.

Nine. One summer, to the village. (Wasn't it the time when, somewhere between Lyon and Valence, he heard a little boy speaking Flemish to a man in a sailor's cap; it threw him a little, but of course Flanders wasn't yet far enough away to allow one to talk to total strangers just because they happened to speak the same language, and apart from that his formal Flemish would have made a conversation difficult; he was already back in his compartment before he realized that what the boy had referred to in Flemish as "the teeyayay" was in fact "the TEE," the *Trans-Europe Express*). Can it be that he has retained no other memory of the last nocturnal hours he spent between one minute past three and a quarter past five, until the blue bus pulled up, save for killing time in and around the station shivering, sleeping, dozing? At first, apart from the occasional fast car or truck, there was no sign of life; even the nightclub was closed, and further away the street where the whores had congregated was deserted. At this ungodly hour he couldn't leave his luggage with anyone, so all strolling was ruled out if his belongings exceeded a light valise. His mouth tasted stale from the cigarettes he had smoked in the dark compartment or in the train corridor, refusing to nod off for fear of missing his stop; because from Lyon onward the name of the station the night train was arriving at wasn't announced over the loudspeakers, probably so as not to disturb the sleeping passengers, and sometimes he had the impression that he was the only traveler getting out in Avignon. In order to wake up what he needed most was something to eat, but it was not until the seventh or ninth journey that he discovered—a long way off to the right on the boulevard that follows the walls on its way to the station—a bar that opened very early, though not before five in the morning. And after that discovery the fresh coffee and croissants of the yawning, probably unwashed owner, and the company of a few other wide-awake customers made him reluctant to test out his regained lucidity in the empty streets. Still, wouldn't he have discovered that the nightclub was closed or found that glossy, brightly colored bar just the same if he had always stayed close to the station? What he hasn't done, what he has not succeeded in doing, is to use the night to explore the town while it's still asleep. He regrets this, but someone who has just had a sleepless nighttime journey of twelve hours or so obviously lacks the enthusiasm or curiosity or expectations that would make such an undertaking fascinating (and how well one understands why a soldier from a besieging army might risk his life, disguised as a monk, a tramp, or a woman, to wander the streets of the stubbornly resisting town, anticipating the day of his victorious entry by weeks or months or years). He might doubt whether he had ever even entered the nocturnal town if he had not retained the memory of how unusual the appearance of another human being was in the hallucinatory, empty labyrinth of its streets: One heard a footstep, and a little further on saw a man appear from a side street on the left and disappear down the one on the right, a ghostly image that made the emptiness of the town even more pronounced, almost tangible; it was a real ordeal to meet someone else: One could hear and see each other coming from a long way off, and suddenly it proved very difficult to walk normally, since the closer one got to the other person the greater one's curiosity became, not to mention that which one presumed the other person was feeling too—simply passing by each other, as could happen with thousands of people, without talking to each other or coming to blows, suddenly seemed so unnatural, so improbable, that one felt relieved when the other person had gone past, as if one had escaped a great danger; and if it was an early-shift worker, still warm from his bed, one could *feel* the bitterness with which the passerby noted that there were obviously still young people in middle-class clothes wandering about the town alone at this impossible hour (the solution was to quicken one's step, as if one were walking somewhere urgently, thus averting this irritation); and when it happened that the other person was walking ahead of one in the same direction, it was better if one stopped for a moment, so that he didn't begin to think he was being stalked; and if one were being followed oneself, one could take the first side street on the left three times in a row and if necessary stop en route—but by doing that you easily begin to look like a conspirator or a terrorist; it was the period of the FLN attacks, when the infamous CRS riot police were patrolling every town by night. An adventure? But no, this town was dizzyingly empty, no adventure was conceivable other than something very short-lived, trivial, and primitive, as in the Stone Age; and his exhaustion was telling him so clearly that he was incapable of rising to any adventure, so that he thought it just as well, if the early-morning bar wasn't open yet, to stay in the station. After all, there were a few interesting things to see there. In the ticketing hall a North African was sleeping next to his knapsack; from the terrace one could see the sky lightening in summer, and for the nocturnal traveler the jewel-like brilliance of the sky was the first sign by which he could recognize the country he had arrived in—because the station was too empty to hear the *accent du midi*, and the only person collecting tickets might as well come from Laon or French Flanders; and then a shy, colorless little woman, who seemed to have materialized out of the twilight, asked him which way to the bus for Digne, and he did nothing more than give her the minimum necessary information—now he can be amazed about it, he can regret not having used such encounters to speak to people: always the same old shyness, the same unnatural diffidence? or was he afraid, demanding as he was, that the other person would prove not to be familiar with such a night, clinging stubbornly to the narrow-minded, stuffy concerns of the previous and the following day? or did he fear most of all that the other person, in daylight, among all the other people would suddenly become dreadfully indifferent to him? or was he just too tired to listen properly, speak properly—let's not forget that his throat was painfully horse from smoking on an empty stomach; on two terrace chairs of the still-closed café on the left-hand corner of the boulevard a tramp was sleeping, and didn't seem to be cold. It was hard to imagine that there were any signs of life in Avignon stirring earlier than those around the station: A man sat down at the café next to the sleeping tramp; a short, shabby-looking man thumped down a pack of papers—*Le Provençal?*—on a pedestal table on the same terrace and disappeared, and the papers just sat there unguarded, anyone taking one left some money next to the pack; a man came cycling along and went into the station; a man walked across the street and stood waiting by the papers, who knew for what, until at last he was picked up by a van. When both hands on the illuminated clock above the station entrance formed a single vertical line—and who knew if the blue bus might not leave earlier today, because of a whim or a mistake of the driver's, or because of a new summer timetable? But it was never until the last minute, or even beyond, that the bus turned into the station square. It never ceased to amaze him that so many people turned up so unexpectedly, one had no idea from where, to board the bus as soon as it appeared—although there were always empty seats. The sleepy driver and conductor had plenty of work stowing packages and cases in the luggage compartment, on the roof. The shy woman was already sitting in one of the front rows.

Ten. The same summer, back to the north; same as last year, he is driven to Avignon, but there are no girls in the back seat; before the train leaves he has time to dine with his kind escort at the buffet, and eight years later he still won't have succeeded in eating another Cantal cheese like that afternoon's. —And only now does it fully dawn on him that he doesn't have an exact grasp of the station's orientation. More precisely: He does now have *some* sense, since a glance at the map of Avignon is sufficient for that, but it's doubtful whether that sense is actually integrated into his experience. At each departure, the observation that the train headed to the left, as seen from the station building, gave him a slightly dizzying feeling of bewilderment. This tallied with the fact that the train to Paris always departed from track one—that is, the track leading off to the left—but each time he couldn't help but feel that the overall direction toward Paris, for anyone standing on the platform with their back to the station, must be to the right. Knowing that the train followed the Rhone as far as Lyon, he obviously imagined that the tracks in the station also ran north-south; that he didn't take into account the station's being located to the west of the tracks can be explained by the improbability of the fact that the bus from Cavaillon, a town south of Avignon, approached the station from the north, and perhaps too by his—unjustified?—conviction that the town lay to the east of the station, and thus on the same side of the tracks. So that, in his mind's eye, he saw, from west to east: the Rhone—the railway parallel to it—the station—the boulevard parallel with it—and then the town. So it must have been that the bus approached the station from the south. But how could he possibly have failed to realize that, according to this plan, the railway ran between the town and the Rhone, for which there was no factual evidence? And how was he able to suppress the uneasiness caused by this realization? Perhaps he attributed the lack of any visible proof to the fact that the attention of the arriving traveler is always focused on non-topographical details? But the paradoxical fact remains that according to his more or less subconscious image of the region, Avignon could not even be called a town on the Rhone. Of course, one glance at the map is sufficient to dispel all incoherence and ambiguity—like waking from an unpleasant dream in which one no longer recognized oneself (reality is formidably simple): The unexpected, "wrong" way in which the train appeared to depart the station was not south, but, at least to begin with, east; and the station was not east, but north of the railway, so south of the town; the railway, running roughly parallel with the Rhone along an approximate northeast to southwest diagonal, encompassed roughly half the circumference of the town; and in fact the bus, which turned onto the boulevard from the southeast, approached the station from east-northeast.

Eleven. On a winter's day, after having spent a few nights in Paris with them (he stayed at the *Hôtel Voltaire*, where Baudelaire once lived), he was accompanied by his family to the *Gare de Lyon*. There awaited the brand-new aluminum Mistral express. Today's leave-taking is reminiscent of the departure of an exile, of a missionary, of a colonist. According to the railway time-table, we will be getting into Dijon at about three-thirty in the afternoon, Lyon at about five, then Valence one hour and Avignon two hours later. He will be spending the night in Avignon, at the *Hôtel Paris-Nice* on the straight street opposite the station, hiring a car for the following day's journey. It's his mother who has urged him to this extravagance, as if the blue bus couldn't have accommodated his large, green, metal suitcase just as well as any car. Is this a decisive departure, a defection? He is going to live in a house south of the village. Forever? Perhaps. How can you predict? Shortly before arriving in the village, his driver gives him a paper knife made of some soft metal, with, printed on the brown handle—a material unknown to him: more metal, but painted?— GAILLARD AVIGNON on one side, and TAXI 81-06-68 on the other. Now he wonders what the man thought of him after help-ing carry his heavy suitcase into the isolated, empty, still only half-habitable house; and from the point of view of the driver he can find no better hypothesis than: a rich man's son who for some mysterious reason has removed himself on a temporary basis from the circle of his family and friends.

Nothing more than a collection of tangents and intersections: *Via Avignon.* An erosion, perhaps? But so much less extensive than that of the Rhone from Sierre in Valais past Geneva and Lyon and Avignon as far as the Camargue. And then he asks shyly: Is it worthwhile noting all this down?—He really should accept once and for all that it's not at all about simply record-ing in a satisfactory way what seems to have happened, and even less about presenting events as if they themselves had oc-curred in a satisfactory way. It's not even about forcing facts, things, events, phenomena to reveal their meanings to us: How quick we would be, then—in secret—to attribute precisely those meanings to them that we cannot seem to find, and which they therefore probably do *not* contain. We live badly, we live unsat-isfactorily; oh well, so what, what are you going to do about it? That's just the way it is, that's just how the material is, the raw material with which we have to make do. This is not a strug-gle with reality, this is not even a struggle with all the slimy, sluggish forces that prevent us from experiencing reality truly awake. This is a naming, a summation, an inventory. Pointless? But not hopeless . . . Though the very act of putting this hope into words could falsify the measurement, the sum in the sense of our wishes. One can write: Events demand to be recorded, objects specified, phenomena revealed. Apart from that it's better to remain silent: calculating, so that not a single effort is lost. In that case, though, the question does arise whether it might not be best to ignore all those notes, those letters, those books of his; whether it might not be best to limit oneself completely to memories. But that would still mean that all sorts of shreds, shards, and splinters would be added—involuntarily—to a few hyperbolic, ultimately not-too-shameful experiences, which, however, would even then only exist on paper: as if these phenomena were being multiplied by one another instead of simply added together; and even if his report succeeded in following his chronology with obsessive scrupulousness, months and perhaps years that would have to remain unrecorded here might nonetheless—unconsciously—illuminate those experiences to be mentioned; anyway, it's probably already too late to do without those documents; he probably consulted them as soon as he was asked about his relationship with Avignon, if only to save himself from any awkward silences. So let's allow him to know what he could easily have deduced from a few books in his library: that it can't be ruled out that his first, very unsatisfactory, in-passing visits to Avignon may actually correspond quite well with the nature of the town. Not only because Avignon was the only obvious rest-stop for all vacationers on their way to Spain or the Mediterranean until 1961—when the great diversion of the *nationale sept*, which runs about six kilometers to the east of the town of Bédarrides, as far as the *Chartreuse de Bonpas*, was completed—but because, since the building of the bridge over the Rhone by Saint Bénezet and his *frères pontifs*, Avignon had never been anything more than a crossroads: from Spain to England via the Perthus Pass and the Rhone Valley; from Rome, Naples, and the Northern Italian towns to Languedoc and Aquitaine along the Via Domitia, the Aude, and the Garonne; from Marseille and Montpellier to the markets of Champagne, Paris, or the Flemish towns. And even the Avignon popes could be said to have arrived in the town only gradually and almost by chance: As Clement V, Bertrand de Got, former archbishop of Bordeaux, spent at least as much time in his native Gascony, or—having convened the Council—in Vienne, and then in Lyon or Carpentras, as in the Dominican monastery of Avignon, and didn't even die in the town on the Rhone, but in Roquemaure, on the other bank, on his way back to his homeland; that Jacques Duèse, John XXII, who even before his elevation to cardinal had also been bishop of Avignon, and thus compelled to remain at his episcopal seat, was planning at the age of eighty-five to settle in Bologna with the Curia—he felt Rome was still too insecure—clearly betrays how provisional he considered his stay; then, when the return to Rome was still too risky for Benedict XII, former Cardinal Jacques Fournier, because of the feud between the Colonnas and Orsinis, and he consequently had the bishop's palace in Avignon rebuilt, the fact that he nonetheless had the roof of St. Peter's repaired in his absence can't have been a simple consolation prize for the Holy

City; and, in the end, it was only Pierre Roger who, as Clement VI, established himself permanently in Avignon, built the second palace, attracted all kinds of artists to the city, and, in 1348—that is, forty-three years after the coronation of Clement V—bought the town of Avignon from Joan of Naples for eighty thousand guilders.

(Let him now look carefully and deliberately at the map and henceforth—anachronistically, but for the sake of clarity—call any streets, boulevards, squares, or gates by those names of which he is only now aware . . . far from Avignon. Schematically, the town wall can be reduced to the perimeter of a rhombus of which the north and south sides follow an east-west direction, and the east and west sides run from south-southwest to north-northeast. The Rhone flows past the north and west sides. The northwest corner is marked by the *Porte du Rhône*; the first, western half of the northern side by the outer avenue, *Boulevard de la Ligne*, as far as the *Porte de la Ligne* in the center of the north side, and then the second half by the *Boulevard Saint-Lazare*; the northeast corner is formed by the *Porte Saint-Lazare* and the eastern outer avenue, *Boulevard Pierre Brossolette*, but this eastern boundary is interrupted, a little less than halfway down, by the *Porte Thiers*, so that the road inside the walls north of that gate is called *Rue du Rempart Thiers* and south of it *Rue du Rempart l'Imbert*; the southeast corner is the *Porte l'Imbert*, the southwest corner the *Porte Saint-Roch,* but that south side contains four other gates, from east to west the *Portail Magnanen*, the *Porte Saint-Michel*, the *Porte de la République*, and the *Porte*

Saint-Charles; from the *Porte l'Imbert* to the *Porte Saint-Michel* the outer avenue is called *Boulevard Gabriel Péri*, from the *Porte Saint-Michel* to the *Porte Saint-Roch* the *Boulevard Estienne d'Orves*; the road inside the walls is called *Rue du Rempart Saint-Roch* from the *Porte Saint-Roch* to the *Porte de la République*, *Avenue Premier Génie* from the *Porte de la République* to the *Porte Saint-Michel*, and *Rue du Rempart Saint-Michel* from the *Porte Saint-Michel* to the *Porte l'Imbert*; the fourth, western side of the rhombus consists of three, approximately equal sections: at the bottom are the outer avenue *Boulevard Saint-Dominique* and inside the walls the *Rue du Rempart Saint-Dominique* as far as the gate of the same name; in the center the *Boulevard de l'Oulle* and the *Rue du Rempart de l'Oulle* as far as the *Porte de l'Oulle*; above the *Boulevard du Rhône*, the *Rue du Rempart du Rhône* as far as the *Porte du Rhône*. The location of the *Porte de la République* more or less coincides with the vertical projection of the *Porte du Rhône* on the south side of the rhombus; the train station is located on the extension of that projected line, south of the *Porte de la République*, separated by a public garden from the *Boulevard Estienne d'Orves*; the railway follows a line parallel with the Rhone in relation to the diagonal from the *Porte Saint-Roch*, so that the Paris train first follows a west-east direction, then turns north and only reaches the bank of the Rhone northeast of the town. The southern two thirds of the vertical projection between *Porte du Rhône* and *Porte de la République* form, from south to north, the *Cours Jean Jaurès*, the *Rue de la République*, and the *Place Clémenceau*; slightly east of the northern third is the *Place du Palais*, east of it the *Palais des Papes*, north of that the *Promenade du Rocher des Doms*. In the northwest the extension of the diagonal from the *Porte l'Imbert* to the *Porte du Rhône* follows the direction of the *Pont Saint-Bénezet*, in the southeast the *Route de Marseille*—the road to Cavaillon, Apt, or Aix and Marseille. The extension southward of a line from the *Place Clémenceau* to the *Porte Saint-Michel* points to the *Boulevard Saint-Ruf*—the way to Tarascon and Saint-Rémy. The westerly extension of a section linking the *Porte Thiers* and the *Porte de l'Oulle* corresponds with the *Pont Saint-Pierre* along which the *nationale cent* leads to Villeneuve and Nîmes. It's difficult to fit any more topographical data into this geometrical plan, given their arbitrary courses and irregular positions.) (To take another, synthetic, intuitive view, the town might be identified with—seen as a frontal cross section—a scarcely three-dimensional model of a female body, in which case the station, the park in front of it, and the *Porte de la République* form the external sex organs, and the *Cours Jean Jaurès*, the *Rue de la République*, and the *Place Clémenceau* the passage through which spermatozoa, blood cells, and mucus might move up and down; the narrow road between the *Place Clémenceau* to the *Place du Palais* represents the neck of the womb, and the womb itself is formed by the large buildings around the *Promenade du Rocher des Doms*: to the west, around the *Porte du Rhône*, the *Ancien Petit Séminaire*, to the south the *Place du Palais*, the church of *Notre-Dame des Doms*, and the *Palais des Papes*, and to the east the prison; the rest of the town may then be roughly, nonspecifically identified with the complex of bones, muscles, nerves, blood vessels . . .)

One Friday in August, laden with a not very heavy knapsack, he leaves the village and takes the afternoon bus of about a quarter past five to Avignon. At about a quarter past seven, the bus turns left from the *Place de l'Imbert* onto the *Boulevard Gabriel Péri*, drives past the *Porte Saint-Michel* down the *Boulevard Estienne d'Orves* to the *Porte de la République*, and there turns left and stops at the station. Annoyed, he walks into the station, but doesn't find the blonde girl he slept with in Paris almost two years ago. Her letters had been vague; originally she was to arrive on Saturday evening at eight minutes past seven, but when she had changed her mind to Friday at the same time, she had, in case they missed each other, also arranged for them to meet the next day at the station at about two o'clock. She had to come from Périgueux, via Toulouse, Montpellier, and Tarascon, which meant that she would be traveling from nine in the morning on. He walks into town through the *Porte de la République* and across *Place Clémenceau* to a western side street, *Rue Molière*, where he asks a woman in the lobby of the *Grand Nouvel Hôtel*—she had mentioned this hotel in her letters—whether a blonde girl has recently booked a room. The woman can't help him. Hesitant, indecisive, he retraces his steps. On the corner of the *Rue Molière* and *Place Clémenceau*, on the pavement past the municipal theater, he virtually bumps into the girl. She had arrived at thirty-one minutes to seven. (*Avignon sent messengers to them, and as soon as they appeared outside the walls, a delegation of barons and burghers received them on bended knees, and offered them the town. "Sir Count of Saint-Gilles," said the leader of this delegation . . . "we humbly beg you and your well-beloved son, being of our own blood and lineage, to accept this our honourable pledge: all Avignon greets you as seigneur, and each of us delivers into your keeping his person and his possessions, the city elders, the public gardens and town gates," etc. The Count lauded the men of Avignon for the way they had welcomed him, and promised them "the high esteem of all Christendom and of your own country; for you are bringing back chivalry, and Joy, and Parage." Father and son now entered the city: There was neither greybeard nor stripling who did not run through the streets for joy, and he who ran the fastest held himself fortunate. Some cried "Toulouse!" in honour of the Count and his son, while others exclaimed "Ah Joy! Henceforth God is with us!"*) They go for supper in an empty restaurant in the square, and because their clothes are too rustic or because despite the décor it's just not a good restaurant, or perhaps in part because of the late hour, they are badly served—but they don't mind. Then they go and book a room each in the respectable but terribly faceless *Hôtel Paris-Nice* in the *Rue de la République*, and after she's calculatedly mussed up the sheets and blankets in her room, the girl—whom he calls Beatrice, although that's not her name—comes over to lay down beside him. There is no outside window in the room, just a hopper window that opens onto the corridor, opposite the bathroom, so that one hears every sound from the guests using it. (What can he say about a night like that? That nothing is so nocturnally perfect as the belly of a virgin? that his stammering brilliance probably left no room for self-sacrifice or nobility? that his lunatic eagerness, which can never be retrieved, now seems linked, in his eyes, to an awkward frivolity and clumsiness?) The next day they pay a brief visit to *Notre-Dame des Doms*, ignore or else can't find the sundial where the spectator's shadow indicates the time, and spend no time thinking about what was written about this place some eighty years previous by a tubercular Dane. Perhaps they descend the steep steps to the bank of the Rhone, but instead of going onto the *Pont Saint-Bénezet*, they walk across the *Pont Saint-Pierre* to the right bank. The river turns out to be unexpectedly wide, the bridge seems to be miles long and there are no pedestrians to be seen. What is the weather like? Clear, warm, dry—otherwise they wouldn't ever have thought of resting, making love, or generally fooling around in the first undergrowth they found on the right bank—if only the vegetation were denser and the spot weren't dangerously unfamiliar. They reach Villeneuve, find, perhaps with the help of the *Guide Bleu*, the *hospice*, where they are shown Enguerrand Charonton's great panel: *Le Couronnement de la Vierge* (or else: walking past the hospice do they happen to find Charonton's painting mentioned in the *Guide Bleu*?). What can be said now about the way they looked then? At the risk of blowing out of all proportion their more or less unconscious, subcutaneous unease: that a glance now at (just a?) reproduction of this painting clearly (suspiciously clearly?) explains the submerged disquiet in his admiration: the monochrome red angels and blue cherubim (as in the work of Jean Fouquet); the light, disconcerting for those familiar with Flemish Primitives, which while it is in complete harmony with the landscape (where the light from *below* is also blinding), but covers the faces of the saved and the saints with an unimaginable evenness like the light of neon bulbs; the symmetrical physiognomic identity of the Father and the Son; and mainly the hierarchical context: the absence of domesticity or charm in the crowned figure, in comparison with so many Flemish Marys—her moon-shaped, slant-eyed face (the same face as that of the Olympian Hera?), her bony, disturbingly long-fingered hands . . . They are also shown a copy of the *Pietà of Villeneuve*. Down empty, cambered, cobbled streets they go the *Chartreuse du Val-de-Bénédiction*. A wide-arched passageway gives onto a peaceful alleyway planted almost like a garden, where a few children are chattering: "A béguinage," thinks the Fleming, but ordinary people live in the little houses. Together with Beatrice he drinks water from the communal pump in the middle of the alley. The entry gate to the *Chartreuse* is on the left at the end of the street, and a friendly, white-haired guide shows them round. But now he remembers very little of the frescos attributed to Giovanetti of Viterbo, and nothing of the tomb of Innocent VI—perhaps it had been moved elsewhere, whether or not temporarily? His clearest memory is of the cells: the hatch through which the monks' food and books were passed; the dark, anything but coarse paneling and the convenient lectern in the library; the high-walled garden: much less a béguinage than the study of a refined, self-sufficient humanist. They enjoy strolling through the monastery cloisters and gardens. He doesn't remember how they got to the *Fort-Saint-André*: whether via the usual way or up the steep path that leads from the back door of the *Chartreuse*. Looking down at the *Chartreuse* from the fortress, he is reminded of Spain by the bare, yellowish, stony slope. Then they walk or drive back to Avignon. (And with painful clarity he knows that he has forgotten something here, that something happened to them or just to him in or near a café in this town—wasn't it at the bus stop? And so, did they actually go back to Avignon by bus? Or was it that the departure time turned out not to suit them? Did he look at a girl in fascination? At some children? All he remembers is that something escapes him.) They have supper in a cheap place in one of the narrow streets leading to the *Place du Palais*. The next day he accompanies the girl to a Sunday Mass in *Saint-Agricol*; when he hears St. Paul's Epistle on the contrast between flesh and spirit it occurs to him that for him the flesh is a much less suspicious stimulus for love than is the spirit. They have a cold lunch on the terrace of a small café in a deserted square planted with trees, probably near the *Ancienne Eglise des Cordeliers* (the once so productive and yet so thwarted and so stigmatized *fratres minores*) or perhaps near the *Chapelle des Pénitents Blancs*. In the *Musée Lapidaire* they look at the Celtic *Guerrier de Vachères* and at the *Tarasque de Noves*. *At that time there was in a forest along the Rhone, between Arles and Avignon, a dragon, half beast and half fish, larger than an ox and longer than a horse; it had teeth as sharp as a sword, and had horns at both ends. It hid in the water, killed the fish, and sank ships . . . This dragon was named after the area, Tarascon . . .* They get there by bus, spend the night there, and then the following day in Beaucaire; on Tuesday they drive to Saint-Rémy, the following day they walk to Les Baux, on Thursday they stroll around the *Plateau des Antiques*, but in *Saint-Paul de Mausole* they aren't allowed to see Van Gogh's room. That evening a bus takes them back to Avignon, and after wandering around for a while they book into the *Hôtel du Centre*, not exactly lousy but certainly very cheap, in, what, the *Rue du Vieux Sextier*? . . . his diary gives *Rue de la Petite Saunerie*, but that's probably a mistake. His memories are so annoyingly vague that one is virtually compelled to follow his diary entries in order. On Friday they visit the *Musée Calvet*—the former *Hôtel de Villeneuve-Martignan*—and there (apart from the bust of Paul Claudel as a boy, done by his sister, about whom the girl tells him that she was madly in love with her teacher Rodin—who by this time had already dismissed his secretary Rilke?) they only take an interest in the Flemish works: Adriaen Brouwer, Joos van Craesbeeck, Ruysdael, Teniers . . . Before they go to their room in the evening, they ask the manager for an alarm clock; he's stone deaf, sits in a back room watching a blaring TV, telling them about his passion for motor racing. They get up very early the next morning and probably meet the blonde girl's dark-haired friend at the station at a quarter past five. Later they visit the *Eglise-Saint-Pierre* together, and spend a long time looking at a bas-relief by Imbert Baochon. Isn't it also that morning that they have a quick look at the *Palais du Roure*? They go no further than the arched passageway where they read famous names on a commemorative plaque. Those who arrive here are swept grandly in the direction of the *Chartreuse de Villeneuve*; he remembers vividly that there in the arched passageway he lies down on one of the stone benches built against the wall—probably meant for tramps and vagrants lining up for handouts—while the two girls go off to buy bread: "I'm a tramp, and soon two compassionate women will bring me a crust of bread." Now one can see these three young people from on high, with the eyes of a giant or a god or the ugly statue of the Virgin Mary on top of the tower of *Notre-Dame des Doms*, as they walk through the streets of Avignon again: Wouldn't it be a waste, wouldn't it be a shame if they were arguing? And yet it had to happen, and it was completely his fault. (It's possible to find an explanation beneath the immediate cause, which seems a little too convenient to be more than a pretext—that is, the unjustified impression that the two girls have been gossiping about him: Is he resentful because he feels utterly at the mercy of these two women, if only because of the courtesy expected of him? or is it thanks to the awareness, culminating now in the concrete presence of her friend, that he has chosen the blonde girl and no one else, that he is committed to *her*, that his choice is *limited* to her?) By chance they enter an exhibition of sacred art in the *Chapelle de l'Oratoire*, and their focused attention reconciles them to some extent. A strange, bearded young man in dark clerical dress, with grubby cuffs, collar, and nails, shows visitors round. Now he thinks: for anyone wanting to explore an unknown town the most important thing is perhaps attention, irrespective of whether the object of that attention has a great deal or very little to do with said town. However pleasant they found the chamber of the *Chartreuse du Val-de-Bénédiction*, it offered little or nothing upon which one's attention could be focused intently and at length; hence, the man who doesn't care to explore Avignon in any other way than by observing the street life from various café terraces may well pass his time more peacefully and pleasantly than other visitors, but he will also—unless this particular town happens to be the only one he intends to observe in this way—need more time to get to know the place, to possess it, to distinguish it once and for all in his memory from other towns. A young man together with two girls spends a summer day in 1961 looking at chalices and ciboria, at tapestries woven by Avignon Carmelites between 1650 and 1771, at a gold-lined embroidered chasuble in purple moiré silk, the rust-colored embroidery of which—a color obtained by winding a silver thread round a red one—is so carefully finished on both sides that it seems entirely outlandish and gratuitous; and thus that young man will never again be able to think of Avignon without invoking the *Très inconnus* exhibition as a proof, as something to hang on to; for him, on the whole, Avignon will henceforth be represented by: a strange, grubby, fanatical man, the completely naked body of Christ on a processional cross from the church at Uchaud; and then an antependium from the cathedral of Vaison, inspired by the Romanesque and embroidered in the eighteenth century by the Carmelites from a convent the location of which—in or near the town?—he does not even know. That evening they must have eaten for the first time in *L'Agneau grillé*, in an alley off the *Rue des Marchands*, a restaurant whose name evokes some luxuriously gastronomic *relais* but is no more than an extremely cheap and lugubrious soup kitchen. Nevertheless, before entering the empty, dark *Rue des Marchands*, they walked across the *Place Clémenceau*, which on this summer Saturday evening is almost completely full of tables and chairs from the surrounding cafés and restaurants; and while it may be that the prices displayed are simply not in line with their meager resources, it is however immediately apparent once more, just as in Dieulefit but now no longer to him alone, how they are naturally but radically separated from the *ordinary* people—mainly young, talking agreeably, drinking, gesticulating, eating. (And now he thinks: A century before, when no one dreamt of going on a voluntary journey without recommendations and introductions in hand to the circles that would receive, initiate, and entertain them in those strange towns, such loneliness was scarcely conceivable; and perhaps in a century's time, when complete strangers will approach and address one another without ever thinking of the existence of some paralyzing barrier between them, it may seem equally inconceivable.) That same evening, while they're resting in their rooms, he makes the blonde girl cry; he feels condemned more irrevocably than he ever could be by contempt or hatred when he sees the frightened, astonished look of the other girl when she comes to pick them up for the *Son et Lumière*. It's more out of duty than anything else that they go to the *Place du Palais*, buy tickets that are not cheap, take their places in a stand among English, Scandinavian, and German tourists, and then look at the façade of the *Palais des Papes* while the floodlights go on and off, listen to pompous music and ponderous commentary. It disappoints him that not a single character appears before them, that everything is probably operated automatically with a tape and timers; and it seems to him that he wouldn't have been able to resist the temptation—since it was clearly just a matter of making an impression on the crowd—of showing at least the silhouette of a pope at one of the arched windows: there wouldn't even have been any need to hire an extra, an articulated lay figure would have been sufficient; but what fascinates him most, all evening, is the sight of the only, simply, annoyingly, illuminated window in the entire façade, probably lit by a mean, barracks-like electric bulb: inside, he thinks aloud, in a room like a guard post, sit malodorous night watchmen, playing cards with their sleeves rolled up, but they have been strictly forbidden to look out of the window during the performance. It's just as well he can make fun of himself and those strutting Frenchmen, it keeps them all entertained, and a reconciliation is brought about—now he'll stay in a good mood for a week. That night the deaf hotel manager forces his way into Beatrice's room: "N'ayez pas peur!"—maintaining that he's looking for a lost jewel or watch; the following morning he'll apologize and tell a long-winded story about an English tourist who'd supposedly lost some sort of jewelry in the hotel and is now trying to hold him liable; the fact that he must in the process have noticed that the blonde girl isn't sleeping in the same room as her friend makes the trio only very moderately embarrassed. They leave for Arles, and the following Thursday they arrive back in Avignon from Aix, but only to take a bus to Fontaine-de-Vaucluse in the afternoon. They set out on a hike from the *Plateau de Vaucluse* to the village at the foot of the *Montagne de Lure*. (They do not stop at Saumane, which is so close to Fontaine-de-Vaucluse: Even if they knew that this was where Sade lived between the ages of five and ten, that it was probably here that whatever unknown, decisive event in his life took place, they would no more visit Saumane for Sade than l'Isle-sur-Sorgue for René Char.) Meanwhile, he is supposed to have behaved so rudely yet again that his girlfriend's friend had to bite her tongue not to give him a piece of her mind. Six days later, Beatrice accompanies her friend, who is returning to Brussels alone, as far as Avignon; when she gets back to the village, she brings with her a slender, three-branched, wrought-iron Henri III candleholder (in French: *une applique-araignée*) for his room, and tells him that at first the antique dealer in the *Rue Joseph Vernet* didn't want to sell it without the accompanying pendant, but at her insistence gave in with the comment: "J'en ferai un autre." The following Tuesday he accompanies the blonde to the quarter-to-eight blue bus. What happened? Certainly it's time for her to be going back north. But in order to catch the quarter-to-eleven evening train in Avignon, surely the girl could just as well have taken the evening bus? and if for some reason she wants to be in Avignon earlier, then isn't it just churlish of him not to spend her last day together with her? With the words he has access to now, he would be able, years later, to explain his shameful uneasiness more or less convincingly; but his diary registers only a collection of all too devious attempts to invent such explanation. Now he can admit that these were little more than pretexts that he used to persuade the girl to leave in the morning, and alone. A French writer who was asked why he hadn't married replied, "Après une semaine je penserais: 'Comment, cette dame est encore là?'" There is something almost alarming in the first, overpowering pleasure of it, which one has craved for so long—as if ordinary, active life has been undermined. But he finds it far more significant—certainly more so than these all too obvious retrospective explanations—that he still hasn't called the blonde girl by her own name. Alone again in the remote house, he starts putting the deserted rooms in order. In order to erase all trace of the person who's been living there with him? But she has left behind her white, very short shorts, which show off her thighs so perfectly. And on that last night she said to him: "I'm afraid this will be the last time I sleep with you." And that morning as he's cleaning up he sees a little mouse traipsing along the wall, and puts down poison for it: This presence too must have made his loneliness much worse. But it isn't until the afternoon, when as before—as if nothing had happened?—he wants to get back to work, that he finds that this solitude, frighteningly different from the one which up till now he had accepted as a fact of life, is unbearable. Then he suddenly closes all windows and doors, and taking nothing but his wallet, he sets off to catch the evening bus to Avignon. He can't know whether the girl has taken an earlier train. And it's on this journey that a young woman gets off the bus somewhere in the open fields, whereupon a dog—recognizable initially as nothing more than a black dot—comes hurtling towards her from a big farm in the distance, and yelps with joy at her feet. As soon as the bus stops in front of Avignon Station, he starts searching the waiting rooms and the buffet, hectically combing the streets and squares as far as *L'Agneau grillé*—in vain. At about eight-thirty he realizes that, if she hasn't already left, she will be boarding the train in a few hours' time, and so he returns to the station, hoping to be able to see her just before she leaves. By coincidence they bump into each other at the entrance, hitting each other hard. He hears that she's spent the day reading in the *Square Agricol Perdiguier*; in the early evening she discovered that she's without her identity card, remembering that she put it in his wallet for safekeeping; she phoned him repeatedly, in vain, and was on the point of hiring a taxi and trying to get to the village and back as soon as possible. What else happened that evening? Perhaps they ate together at *L'Agneau grillé*, but the rest of the time they spend at the buffet. He is able to say things to her that he would have had to write or else keep from her with regret. Is there a gross distortion in the assertion that she shares in only a very melancholy way his joy at having found her after all? that the alternating joy, resentment, and relief in him are in combination very close to some form of ultimate heartlessness? Before the train glides out of the station he is able to kiss her fingers three times. He no longer remembers how he spent the rest of the night. Remembering their unlikely meeting makes the separation bearable for him. But the first letter she writes him, over a month later and only after repeated insistence on his side—and by way of apology she first sends him a package of sweets—will begin with the words: "I haven't written to you because I'm not doing very well at all."

Will he even now maintain that he has little or nothing to do with Avignon? Experiences like the one mentioned above cannot be had without changing the perception of the space in which they were acquired, and likewise the name of that space. Whether or not he will make time and room in his selfish life for the blonde girl, no one can deny that his decision, or lack of one, at least originates in Avignon. So that one can justly claim that his life is to some extent, in a certain sense, perhaps unsatisfactorily, but nonetheless irrevocably, intertwined with Avignon. And in that case it would not be wide of the mark to see a symptom of this entwinement in the fact that from now on his arrivals in the city are noted explicitly and sometimes at length in his diaries—as if Avignon at last meant enough to him. (And note in how many ways apart from "end up" or "reach a destination" the verb *arrive* is used: someone arrives at a conclusion or an agreement; a baby arrives, a letter, news, an ambitious politician . . .).

(Thirteen.) The second Thursday of the following December he walks to the bus stop near the village. There had been a frost that night, a strong mistral is blowing (and that means the sky is an immaculate, crystal-clear blue), and the bells start ringing as he walks through the village. (Since the departure of the blonde girl for the north he watched autumn descending on the region; he helped a neighbor—he's sorry now to have to admit it, but: unwillingly—with the grape harvest; he ate his fill of the mushrooms that the farmer brought for him, and once he was given so many truffles that his omelet contained more truffle than egg; and a newly arrived blonde girl of about fifteen who has started spending her weekends in the village has thrown him into such violent confusion that he's found himself trembling because of such innocent—or maybe not so innocent?—actions as her looking at him on the street, standing next to him in church; so violent, in fact, that at one point he's on the verge of thrusting a secret note suggesting a rendezvous into her hand—only pride prevented him, and then fear that she would use such a confession to embarrass him; he has received his monthly allowance of three thousand francs from his parents, but though this sum doesn't allow him to go down to the village more than three times a week for a full meal, he's still managed to buy a few books; for example, he's been reading the Marquis de Sade, and with astonishment has observed perhaps for the first time how utterly alien a fellow human being can be: However much his lustful bachelor's life may be haunted by dreams of dissipation, he can't really imagine that he would ever derive any pleasure from cruelty and pain—he's never felt anything in response to tears but resentment, fear, revulsion; from Brussels the blonde girl has sent him a big jar of gherkins and onions that she had pickled "one day when I wasn't really angry, just sad," but her three letters, because of the bitterness expressed in them, as well as her melancholy vulnerability, have made him feel guilty and suspicious; the woods of squat-trunked oaks—*les roures*—have colored all the hills an even red, while the red of the vine leaves is quite bright.) At about ten-thirty he arrives in Avignon, the train to Paris leaves at a quarter to. At first he had considered hitch-hiking north; but the thought of the girl who he would see again up there—and immediately it was as clear as day that she was the only adequate reason for his embarking on the journey—the sudden realization that a meeting with her depended entirely on him, suddenly made everything that might hamper or delay or throw doubt on this brief reunion utterly intolerable. Because even the smooth, infallible train tracks are no longer sufficiently reliable to ward off all concern; he knows very well what he is leaving behind, but not what awaits him in Brussels—this journey is a wager, a ruthless investment. Thus it need not be any cause for surprise that he reads a Simenon novel during the journey, the thing is to put off, or appease, this restlessness for as long as possible. In Saint Rambert d'Albon he sees the first snow of the year. Because the evening TEE is fully booked he will have to wait four hours for the night train. Strolling as far as Pigalle, he's amazed, both at the new, bourgeois elegance of some prostitutes and at the calmness with which he declines their services. But (because desire never ceases to rear its head, never abates except precisely to enthrall him all the more unexpectedly, all the more powerfully) in the dark compartment of the night train he will spend hours with his teeth almost chattering with desire for the not particularly pretty but well made-up girl on the right of the seat opposite him, and only by way of words—when the short fat man in black directly opposite him tells him that he is chief cook on a ship and is now being sent back to Denmark for smuggling, and the girl says that she's traveling to Rotterdam or Antwerp to embark on a ship as an interpreter and stewardess—only as a result of such everyday words will he be brought back to his senses, back to ordinary, everyday reality. He will arrive at Brussels South at six in the morning, have breakfast, book a hotel room, phone the blonde girl's friend and ask her to let her know he's arrived, and sleep until he is woken by her.

(Fourteen.) Ten days later he returns to the south. Obviously he's been able to patch it all up, or a lot of it, with the blonde girl? And is it not from this point that he should call her by her real name? He doesn't have the faintest idea that this is the last time he'll take the train to Avignon alone to go to the village. Isn't it during that journey that after a long hesitation he strikes up a conversation in the corridor with a suntanned girl? and learns that she lives on a Galapagos island? And it's also on this trip that he almost misses his stop: It's dark, the train stops in a station, he gets off to drink some water from a tap, then asks a railway worker who's tapping each wheel (he doesn't know why: do they have to check whether any wheels have cracked? if the brakes are tight or loose?) with a long-handled hammer if this is Valence, but the answer is "Avignon," and so he has just enough time to rush back onto the train and grab his suitcase and say a fleeting good-bye to the suntanned girl. The train is running very late—it seems some electric cables have snapped, they're not sure if it's an act of sabotage or a fault—so that he doesn't catch the morning bus to the village. He books a room in the *Hôtel Paris-Nord*—probably he's too tired to walk to the *Hôtel du Centre*—and sleeps till afternoon. He might as well let the evening bus go without him because he doesn't want to arrive in the village after sunset. For the first time he ventures into an elegant café in the *Rue de la République*—but it's only *Le Régence*, a cavernous drinking emporium with a glazed-in terrace, visibly aimed more at tourists than at the residents of Avignon, and consequently almost empty on this December afternoon, while in the snack bar-cum-dancehall on the corner of the *Rue du Collège d'Annecy* or *des Ortolans* or *Vialla* or perhaps *Saint-Agricol,* young townspeople—dark-haired, white-shirted young men and surprisingly elegant girls—are already crowding together. Smartly dressed women are doing their autumn shopping. It may be freezing, but the sun is shining, and the bare plane trees are casting curious shadows on the pavement. How unusual this town seems in the crystal-clear December light, and naked too, because the traffic is once more proportionate to the dimensions of the town, because a walker is no longer overwhelmed by the always unexpected big-city crowds flooding its streets, because the broad leaves of the plane trees—like decorations taken down once the tourists have gone—no longer shade you from the merciless sky; and one can hardly believe that the tourists one does still encounter—behind the net curtains of the *Hôtel Crillon* or *Savoy* or *Regina*, for instance—could possibly come from too far away—America, Asia, or Australia—so that their presence now feels as historically appropriate as that of the *Palais des Papes*, as necessary as that of the town dignitaries. One should let oneself stare at such an outrageously transparent town for hours and days, one should be able to absorb that mathematically lucid structure once and for all. But he is twenty-four and knowing that in Brussels there is a girl who would like nothing better than make love and play and sleep with him isn't enough, the thought that in this town there are beautiful young women who would also like to have sex with him gnaws at his body. Actually he hopes, expects, is waiting for one of those young women to notice him as he strolls by, to make advances to him. Is he out of his mind? He knows only too well that he'll never get to the point of addressing a woman himself, that he's too irremediably shy for that, too "polite" *and* too proud—too proud to beg or pay the price of feigned enthusiasm or jovial lightheartedness for lust's sake. So it's surely absolutely ridiculous to expect a woman to simply drop into his lap on the quiet, half-empty terrace of the *Régence*, where any overture would echo as if on an enormous sounding board, when the friendly bustle in the dance hall a few blocks away is bound, on the contrary, to favor all sorts of advances? But he quite simply doesn't dare go in that other place; it seems perfectly natural to him—obviously he imagines that everyone else is as self-centered as he—that the inhabitants of this town, so swamped with tourists every year, anxiously exclude these same tourists from their entertainments; that, even before he was able to mention he was staying in the village, they would force him out with their hostile glares—some vulgar, oversexed kid just looking for a good time. He sits there watching the women, perhaps his eyes betray his vertiginous longing for their bodies? Let's hope not. (And now he can clarify: What I was longing for at the time, consciously but hopelessly, was an encounter with a Réa or a Hansi; but perhaps nothing happens to one except what one doesn't expect, and my desire would have put a Réa or a Hansi to flight, not just because it was improper, but largely out of schadenfreude, and likewise because they—and perhaps all women—are less interested in satisfying desire than awakening it.) Feeling terrible about the lonely night to come, he goes to the soup kitchen to eat. At the table opposite his sits a man alone, but the black-haired woman at the next table on the right—on the man's left—did she come in before him or after him? She's eating alone, he's able to have a good look at her. At first he may have thought: no great beauty. But soon he acknowledged that her body is fascinating, particularly its tired face, which would only need a little makeup to be as mesmerizing as the most unattainable actress. And the fact that she may be six years or so older than him only makes him a little more hopelessly shy: a young thing who only thinks about necking, sneaking a few sentimental embraces, about an evening out with a new guy, tantalizingly unfamiliar to her girlfriends, could never live up to his far from impertinent but nonetheless unambiguous desires. The meal becomes one long trembling, panicky tangle of doubts: "You're going to do it. You're not going to do it. You don't dare. I do dare." The most important thing is to stretch out his supper until the man opposite leaves—because he could never speak to her in the presence of a curious, smirking, ironic, or irritated witness—so that it's just as well that the owner keeps disappearing into the kitchen. But will *she* leave, and too soon? Olive complexion, dark hair: the type that interests him immediately; signs of tiredness make her face tragic—and isn't that precisely what he subconsciously wants: a dogged, merciless, desperate pleasure? Sometimes she looks at him, and because he is the way he is, he manages to deduce nothing whatever from this fact. Isn't she also eating unusually slowly? For all he knows it's because she doesn't want to be too early for a rendezvous, or so she can hang around and chat with the owner. Actually, despite everything, he still longs for her to make the first move, to say something to him. But then he's finished dessert, so he orders an espresso, and afterward, perhaps—just to delay his departure—a glass of cognac or marc. And then no more delay is possible, and he must speak up or slink off. What did he murmur, mumble? Is she free that evening? And she, in an amazingly matter-of-fact voice: "J'allais vous demander la même chose . . ." (Please note one thing: that nothing until this moment has ever been able to get him to address a stranger who wasn't a salesperson or café-owner or hotel manager, to appeal to someone else as a fellow-human being, no, nothing except a helpless, embarrassed desire, which his equals and fellow countrymen could never admit to.) For a while they sit and talk together at his table (does that mean she came and sat with him? or was she walking past his table to the door when he spoke to her?), then she suggests going to the cinema. (A relief: She is not proposing any hugely expensive entertainments—but also suspicion: is there any better place in Avignon for getting up to something untoward?) What does he learn about her? That her name is Jacqueline, that she is divorced, has a child; that she is a waitress in a restaurant, not in town (where? in Le Thor? Coustellet? Plan d'Orgon? or at the crossroads near the *Chartreuse de Bonpas*—not that he remembered the latter at the time, but now he remembers at some point driving over the crossroads and thinking: this must be where Jacqueline works); that she had Tuesdays off. Clearer, more significant (but signifying what?) is the way she keeps interrupting herself: "Mais écoute un peu, fais attention, écoute-moi bien . . ." like someone who needs a long build-up in order to be able to choose the right words with all the more care; or like a dying person wanting to give their last words exceptional weight; or like a drunk who needs a little time to find the right formulation in order to make a message clear; or like a not yet fully mature girl used as a go-between by two grown-ups, and who through her exaggerated panting and her solemn expression and the use of a first few clichés picked up by eavesdropping on said grown-ups reminds them that she must no longer be treated as a child, that she is now acting on *behalf* of grown-ups, no longer just playing at being grown up. And, for that matter, what Jacqueline says after these introductions is invariably amazingly stupid or irrelevant—as if she keeps changing her mind at the last moment, holding back something more decisive? or as if all she'd really wanted was to make sure she had his undivided attention? Arm in arm like two good friends they approach the cinema on the *Rue de la République* or *Cours Jean Jaurès*; he probably suggested a drink in the *Régence*, for instance, but she didn't accept, and even as they crossed the street she said she was afraid of being seen in his company by people she knew (he thinks he believed her at the time; and now, looking back, he may think: Nowhere better than in such a concern could I have recognized the town as it really is; and no one better than Jacqueline could have revealed Avignon to me as—among other things—an ordinary French town; but my mind would have needed to be less clouded by desire to notice). The film—a cheap, impossibly ambitious adventure movie with Chinese villains and a real dandy in the lead, her favorite star, who she says looks like him—is stupid enough for him to devote all his attention to her. But she's watching. He puts an arm round her waist, he wants to kiss and cuddle. Both annoyed and concerned, he feels that there's a bandage around one of her thighs—"Oh yes," he thinks, "a waitress." But it surprises him that she makes things so difficult for him, that she remains so inaccessibly hunched over, scarcely responds, if at all, to his caresses, doesn't turn to face him except to ask a question about his job, money, parents, as though despite her gaze being fixed on the screen her mind after all was on other things entirely. He loses heart, stops cuddling, tries to watch the film in a cool, detached way; and it's not improbable that he's misunderstood her intransigence; only years later will he see a male wagtail dancing for an immobile, almost paralyzed female, and see at last in that frozen state the possibility of great desire. How else to interpret the sentence that Jacqueline whispers in his ear shortly afterward: "Tu dois bien faire l'amour," or: "Tu dois bien savoir faire l'amour, toi"? What could be meant by this? To what is it the prelude? And is it surprising that he should at the time have interpreted this raising of a subject not yet mentioned as a prospect, a promise? When perhaps she means nothing more than that she wants him to caress her again? And what does he reply? "Peut-être bien," or "Je ne sais pas," or "J'espère"? But he certainly doesn't say that he's never made love to an experienced woman before. Probably he asks her why she said this, but she doesn't reply, or else is evasive. What else could he think about except what may, what must soon happen? And then the film is over, and in the brightly lit foyer she says she thought it was really good, and it's quite possible that he agrees with her out of cowardly stupidity, or simply mindlessly, instead of saying that he'd hardly paid attention, since the film was garbage. She declines the offer of going for another drink, and also—not at all indignantly: rather regretfully and apologetically, in fact—the suggestion of going to a hotel. What should he do now? He walks with her to the *Rue J. H.*

Fabre, but soon she asks him to leave her, she doesn't want him to accompany her to her door—because of the neighbors—and she can't let him in because of the child. So they part, at a threshold which is not hers. They kiss, not very passionately, fleetingly, self-conscious. She says to him—or did she do so earlier in the evening?—that he'll be able to find her every Tuesday evening at *L'Agneau grillé.* And then he lets her walk on alone, docile, without making a fuss, without making threats, as befits a well-brought-up young man, and he walks back to the hotel, surprised at the contradiction between her behavior and that whispered sentence, very much doubting whether she'll ever prove more eager in the future, obviously not even thinking of asking for her address, or following her at a distance to see where she lives. So he goes to bed for want of anything else to do. The next day he leaves for the village on the morning bus, but the very next day he undertakes a short business trip to Marseille, Toulon, and Hyères for his parents, and does not return to the village before Saturday. (How does one express the desire of a lonely twenty-four-year-old? One evening at about ten-thirty he bumps into three very young, beautifully made-up girls in an empty avenue, they look at him shamelessly, cooing and clucking as they approach—and he isn't capable of doing anything but clenching his fists and thinking: If I were to do now what they fear and long for, then *I* would be the dirty pervert who even accosts underage girls—the letch that they can all run away from, dying with laughter.)

(Fifteen.) Astonishingly, it takes seven weeks before the temptation of spending a Tuesday evening in Avignon becomes too much for him. Most probably it was only the dangerous obligation implied by a second meeting that restrained him so long (but he has not yet suspected Jacqueline of the least calculation); what finally drives him to Avignon in the end is the feeling that he must be the last man on earth who refrains, regretfully, from sexual misconduct. He approaches Avignon like a satyr, determined to go to bed with Jacqueline at all costs. But she isn't at the soup kitchen, and in answer to his question the café owner replies gruffly: "Il y a longtemps qu'elle ne vient plus, celle-là." So why shouldn't he curse those seven chaste weeks? and his modesty, which has made Jacqueline unattainable forever? It turns into a grim evening of wandering around, and sometimes he stops, desperately out of breath, thinking: For heaven's sake, let a woman talk to me, so she can see by looking at me that I'd like nothing better than to ask to lick her all over, let her pay me for it like a whore—I just know that there must be beautiful women out there who beg unwilling young men to spend a single night with them, so why not me? He has forgotten now whether it's coincidental that he enters the narrow *Rue Aubanel* and *Rue Bancasse*, whether he goes just to enjoy the exciting propositions of the prostitutes; but both streets are empty, obviously the whores have left town along with the tourists. And the solitary shivering woman enveloped in a fur coat who in response to his—helpless? lecherous? crazed?—look slows down and smiles at him? At first he almost thinks her a figment of his frantic, morbid desires; but then words and numbers are pronounced that remove all doubt: he has accosted the last whore in Avignon. It's with a kind of dull resignation that he follows her to a hotel (the same one where he had sometimes seen an old woman—she often sat at an open window on the ground floor—whose presence was explicable only by theorizing some inconceivably gruesome form of prostitution), with a kind of fear of seeming impolite otherwise, ungrateful for the fact that she has—after all—guessed at his misery. He doesn't bat an eye at the fuss about the room, the towels, since he knows this is how things are done; but in the room he averts his gaze from her depressingly low, slack buttocks, and ensures he makes love to her in such a way that he does not see her face. How essentially irrelevant that fumbling around remains in relation to his desire is apparent from the fact that that same night in a room in the *Hôtel du Centre* he will masturbate repeatedly, as grimly as a hermit chastising himself. On the morning bus to the village there's a girl of about ten, and a woman who—apart from the blonde hair—but it could be dyed?—looks disconcertingly like Jacqueline; a likeness that he would have dismissed easily as a hallucination, a result of his tiredness and obsession, if she had not, whenever he turned in fascination to look at her, smiled with a kind of melancholy forbearance, as if she wanted to speak to him but that this was impossible because of the child; he doesn't dare ask her if she isn't perhaps Jacqueline. A week later he will discover some itchy pustules on the head of his penis.

(Sixteen.) When, some six weeks later, on a Saturday afternoon, he leaves the village, he has no inkling that it will be the last time that he undertakes the journey from the Provençal village to Brussels alone. But it's clear from his diary that he is now finally able—because he is sufficiently familiar with the journey? or perhaps because something in him suspects that he won't be making the trip all that often anymore?—to devote adequate attention to his fellow passengers. Again a woman resembling Jacqueline is sitting in the blue bus—or just another woman who looks like her?—this time with a little boy beside her, and she goes only as far as Apt. There's a handsome boy who remains standing, next to the driver, who at a stop in a village sees a friend of his, roller-skating on the road, and he leans out of the open door to shout out to him, and the other boy gives a cheerful wave and comes over to the door; but they don't say much, just look at each other and smile, and only when the bus starts up do they yell something at each other; at the stop in Viens, the village on top of a steep hill to the right of the road, the boy gets off, walks over to three men who are standing waiting by a car—his father, an elder brother, and perhaps an uncle?—and embraces each of them; probably he has come from the "asylum" in Digne or further away to spend the weekend at home. As far as Avignon he can look at the young, ostentatiously dressed and made-up woman in front of him to the left, who fusses with her lips as soon as she feels him watching her; he immediately thinks she may be a whore who's still getting used to her trade, doesn't consider that she might be an ordinary woman from a village or small town wearing makeup for the very first time. What he wouldn't give to hear why all those people have boarded the blue bus, whether their hearts race as they enter Avignon, and why. But it's perfectly possible that once in the station he doesn't pay the least attention to all those French travelers waiting for trains who used to fascinate and engage him: They're all sitting around and by the look of it have been doing so for hours, the woman in black, the man with the white moustache, obviously the railway only has long layovers, perhaps it's because they can get a good price this way (like the old farming couple in the village, whose son works at the station) that they all prefer to have their trips take two or three times as long than if they took the bus; and however unmistakably white and Western they may be, their eyes all express the same essentially timid, rather hangdog expression, and that man's limply dangling hand the same slavish resignation, as the much poorer North African underclass (negotiations are being held in Evian; in Algiers there is street fighting between the French army and the OAS) who a short distance away are sitting or lying on the ground or on their scanty luggage: *traveling is a disaster*. He may be the poorest of them all—he had to borrow three thousand francs from the postman in the village to be able to leave: when he gets to Paris all he'll be able to buy is an espresso, and in Brussels he'll have to change his last coins to buy a tram ticket—but because of the smoothness and ease with which he now enters the station, because he is able quickly to find a half-empty compartment in the train when it arrives, he belongs to another race entirely, including both the staff in the restaurant cars (who serve tea between Ventimiglia and Menton, and supper between Menton and Marseille) and the businessmen (for whom from 1967 onward a separate office carriage will be attached to the Mistral, so that they can use the ten or so hours of the journey for dealing with urgent business). He is even, for the first time, despite the presence of three other passengers in the compartment, able to fall asleep huddled on his seat. On the morning train from Paris to Brussels, he will have, from Mons onward, a conversation with a Pole who has lived in France since 1942. (In Brussels he will see the blonde girl walking in the street from the tram, get off the tram, run after her but then walk past her with feigned casualness—but she will catch hold of his coattail. They will decide to get married.)

(This is already the beginning of the end. His return to the south, a few weeks later, is in a car, with his parents and his sister; they skirt Avignon to the east, make a brief stop in the village with the two churches, since the final destination of the journey is the peninsula near Hyères. Three and a half months later, in order to marry the blonde girl, he takes the train north, no more than following a tangent past Avignon, the line that passes through the station in an elegant arc. The car that later brings him with his blonde wife from a town in Lorraine to Hyères will of course skirt Avignon as well, along the new route of the *nationale sept* (via Védène, Jonquerettes, and Chateauneuf-de-Gadagne). Later they will spend a few days in the village.)

(Seventeen.) From the village they set out for Avignon one Tuesday morning on the blue bus. When the two of them arrive together for the first time in the town—the streets are unrecognizably and dizzyingly colorful for anyone who's only seen them in December—they are met—somewhere in the *Cours Jean Jaurès*, which seems incomprehensibly narrow?—by a car that takes them to a chateau near Vaison. (And it's during this stay in Vaison that they make an excursion to Nyons, and he, while his wife is buying a black-and-white frock with Greek motifs, recognizes the *Place du Docteur Roux* only gradually as the square he entered some five years before as a tramp, astonished that neither the name Nyons nor the characteristic square were sufficient to jolt his memory at once.)

(Eighteen.) But—unfortunately?—the next arrival in Avignon remains unforgettable, on the way back to Belgium from Vaison. The route that the bus follows past afternoon fields and vineyards seems dull and interminable, he forgets where the two girls got on: his memory of a village on top of a barren hill, at the foot of which the bus stops, strikes him as unreliable. The girls are both so slender, their skin is so dark that he would take them for gypsies if they weren't so unconventionally dressed in baggy sweaters and tight slacks—or perhaps colorful, sloppy but short dresses. The charming, not even especially provocative way they chomp on their chewing gum and look at the passengers, everything about them makes ordinary people feel threatened, demolished, decayed. Sisters? Poor village girls on their way to a night out in the nearby town? But have poor girls ever been able to wear clothes this shabby with such self-satisfaction? Or perhaps they're town girls leaving the dreary holiday village? In Avignon they get off at one of the first gates after the *Route du Pontet*; one of the girls is barefoot, holding her sandals in her hand, or perhaps she only puts her sandals on then. At that moment his wife has already told him about the man from the Walloon provincial town who, on his honeymoon in Paris, was waved at by a prostitute, asked his wife to wait for him, and never came back: what might not have happened if one of the girls had beckoned to him? But when he lets his lecherous curiosity play out in his mind, the two girls eventually arrive at a house, and what is there left for him to do but stop stalking them? Apart from that, they're both far too knowing not to send him packing with their sarcasm long before he reached that point. And so they disappear forever down the *Rue Salengro* or *Rue Puy*, it's Sunday, perhaps they spent the week with relations in the country? He still knows nothing about the so-called good girls who spend their holidays in Saint-Tropez, underwritten by naïve rich patrons, always defending their "honor" by pretending to be lesbians, though perhaps not irredeemably so; but the unassailable frankness of *these* girls—and perhaps too his unconscious association of the streets of Avignon with the mythical labyrinth—make him almost automatically identify their destination with some scandalous, indecent deed: as though they would break in somewhere this evening, or else undress and fondle each other for some rich goggle-eyed sucker, who can then be blackmailed afterward; it would surprise him less than finding out that they were hoping to prostitute themselves—he finds them still too lively and unconventional for that, not passive enough. He spends that night sleeping on a suitcase, in the corridor of the over-crowded train; with some difficulty his wife has managed to find a seat in a first-class compartment; the image of the two young girls is indelible and sears his consciousness.

The following spring the journey is to Hyères via Toulon, they have booked couchettes (two top beds; they sometimes hold hands across the gangway) so that they swish past Avignon asleep. But (nineteen) they return from the village on the evening bus. In Avignon they have to wait for the train until shortly before midnight, and so go to the movies. But once he's got into his couchette the film turns out not only to have killed time but also to have aroused the familiar, absurd desire: as on the previous journey back, with the two girls on the bus, he is now bewitched by the image of the girl who appeared naked and swaying her hips, asking a man, pouting, "Tu me trouves bien?" He doesn't sleep that night. In the morning at the *Gare de Lyon* he watches in bewilderment and admiration the departure of the young woman, who, whether or not asleep, lay motionless all night in the bottom couchette and now, serenely, with not a hair out of place, without a single crease in her gray suit, walks toward the exit as though she's just left home and will shortly be getting straight down to work.

(Twenty.) Then comes summer. For the first time they go from the town in Lorraine via Brussels and Avignon to the Provençal village. Nevertheless, he can't think of anything more significant to say about the journey than that from the bus taking them from the *Gare du Nord* to the *Gare de Lyon* he sees, on a terrace in the *Boulevard Saint-Germain*, a skinny, model-like girl with dark makeup, roaring with laughter, and is offended by that laughter; that during the journey he reads most of a novel by Hugo Claus; that one Monday they are still in Brussels and the next Wednesday in the village. He isn't even sure whether they sit or lie down from Paris to Avignon—it seems to him that they didn't book couchettes this time—or whether they arrived in Avignon at night or during the day. (Notice how Avignon gradually blurs, even becomes less an arrival than a departure point, or, even more neutrally: simply a set of coordinates from which to plot a course.)

(Twenty-one.) He can say even less about the return, a month and a half later. It must have been on the last Tuesday in August, but in his diary the journey is not expressly mentioned. His blonde wife is pregnant but they don't know that yet. Nor do they know that this is their last arrival in Avignon, at least for about five years, and perhaps forever. As if fate, for the sake of a mysterious symmetry, had contrived to make his final arrivals in Avignon as vague in his memory as his first.

This is Avignon? That's how his Avignon is. A collection of streets that proceed at the speed of a pedestrian in a hurry, of boulevards that glide past at the speed of a bus; a town that revolves like a turntable with the increasing or decreasing speed of an arriving or departing train (around what point of rotation? No place seems to him so motionless, unvarying, frozen, as the *Chartreuse du Val de Bénédiction,* situated outside the town on the opposite bank; but what about the *Palais des Papes?*). Not even a turntable: nothing but a crossroads; a point of intersection without any surface area leading from Spain to the Low Countries. *The Rhone valley is the principal break and natural means of communication between the Mediterranean and northern Europe. In the early fourteenth century it connected the two great economic centres of Christendom, that is, central and northern Italy with Flanders: and it connected the great political centres, London and Paris, with Rome and Naples . . . consequently, since it was well south of Vienne (90 miles), stopping there did not mean an unnecessary diversion of route for those coming by land from Italy and intending to proceed on to Spain, Aquitaine or Langeudoc. Avignon was also nearer the sea. Its bridge was the famous Pont Saint-Bénezet, the building of which between 1177 and 1185 became the subject of legend, and across it ran the ancient Roman road, the Via Domitia, which had no other way over the Rhone since the ruin of the ancient Roman bridge at Arles. Since that bridge had collapsed the bridge of Avignon was the southernmost to cross the Rhone before it reached the sea. Consequently Avignon reaped the advantages that came from the trade of the estuary.* In brief: an intersection, a node of lines of force? And scarcely an object itself? But a point that nevertheless at one stage expanded until it had a surface area, and one which is in fact surrounded by various walls, growing longer and longer. And hence a space after all, to be entered, built upon, inhabited, abandoned, demolished; a space that classifies mankind: one is either born in or outside it, one will die there or elsewhere, one has entered it or not. How little of all this is apparent from the way he has stopped in at this town, from the way he's used it. His belief that one's failure to take notice of certain things is less grave, less hopeless a lapse than not to have made oneself noticed by them—and yet, how soon the traces we leave stand revealed as nothing more than distortions, mutilations—this belief offers little consolation. The station, *Chapelle de l'Oratoire, Eglise Saint-Agricol,* the corner of the *Rue Molière* and the *Place Clémenceau,* a little hotel in the *Rue du Vieux Sextier,* a soup kitchen north of *Saint-Didier,* the *Rue Fabre* and the movie theater almost directly opposite, an early-morning café near the *Porte l'Imbert*: Avignon would be reduced to a very cursory topography indeed if one limited the town to those places and buildings that he acknowledges have left traces in his life. The following have only scarcely, or poorly, certainly not unforgettably, been entered or viewed: *Musée Calvet, Musée Lapidaire, Pont Saint-Bénezet, Notre-Dame des Doms, Saint-Didier.* And then, places about which he draws a complete blank, names which project not a single image: *Eglise des Cordeliers, Chapelle des Pénitents Gris, Hôtel Crillon, Chapelle des Pénitents Blancs, Synagogue, Chapelle de la Visitation, Chapelle des Pénitents Noirs, Tour Saint-Jean, Saint-Symphorien.* And then, above all, a hiatus, a deep hole in the fourth dimension—that building, hard to ignore, of which he has seen only the unrestored front façade; which, indeed, he saw for longer than he really wanted (which in no way mitigates his inexplicable irritation at the nineteenth-century restoration elsewhere): the *Palais des Papes*, which he has never entered, more than fifteen thousand square meters in size, of which Rilke wrote from Paris on October 23, 1909 to "Liebe Lou": "*Almost daily, for seventeen days, I saw the immense Papal Palace, that hermetically sealed castle, in which the Papacy, finding itself going bad at the edges, thought to conserve itself, boiling itself down in a last genuine passion. However often one sees that desperate house, it stands upon a rock of unlikelihood, and one can enter it only by a leap over everything traditional and credible.*" Is there even a prospect, a chance that we will one day fully understand things? Now he can express the hypothesis that the ring—within the present walls of the city and indeed touching them by means of the Promenade—formed by the *Rue des Trois Colombes, Rue Campane, Paulain, Philonarde, des Lices, Fabre, Joseph Vernet*, and *Grande Fusterie*, probably follows the line of an earlier fortification: but this idea was only inspired by a glance at a map of the town—when he was walking down the same streets, the thought never occurred to him. And he has to admit that, even with the help of his diary, it's impossible for him to work out when he entered Avignon proper for the very first time, when he first went through the town gates. It's obviously to make up a little for this strange forgetfulness and lack of attention (as long as no desirable woman happened to appear, who would then demand excessive, completely disproportionate attention) that he now mentions a large, yellow square sloping to the left over which he walked with . . . the blonde girl? He no longer remembers when it happened—was the blonde girl's friend present?—and when he now tries to point out the spot on the map, his finger hesitates between a peculiar, unnamed district near where the *Rues Grande Fusterie, des Grottes,* and *de la Balance* almost collide, and then further north, in front of the *Ancien Petit Séminaire*: the square was empty, the houses seemed almost derelict, there was a very small, unattractive café, of which it was hard to say whether it was temporarily closed or had been abandoned permanently; a few people were sitting on the pavement, but he maintains that it was impossible to determine whether they were vagrants simply having a rest, or the poor inhabitants of those houses behind them. Probably this is the same feeling of inadequacy that leads him one morning to bring along a large double sheet of squared paper: the first, third, and fourth pages are divided into unequal columns, the first, narrowest one, contains nothing but dates, the second a concise list of Avignon facts and names, and the third, less wide than the previous one, other facts that are also important but have little or only indirect relevance to Avignon. Everything is noted down with a rather obsessive neatness—probably there was a rough draft first—the homework of an industrious if not very intelligent pupil. One wouldn't really know how to go about reading this table if he didn't explain that it's bound to be very incomplete, since it wasn't drawn up using some *History of Avignon* or other, but only relying on books already in his possession in which there happens to be a mention, and usually only a passing mention at that, of Avignon. It seems that he's finally understood the purpose of this text, and even approves. This offers the opportunity to mention fragments of another, deeper past, to write what he could and should have been aware of, concerning Avignon, while he was staying there, and what he now—hopefully—knows once and for all:

Avenio: a high cliff on the Rhone, for the Celts and later for the Romans a point of strategic value. From 1177 to 1185, eight years, Bénezet and his *frères pontifs* work on the construction of the bridge over the river: a time when the building of a bridge justified the founding of a religious brotherhood, when holiness focused mainly on bringing order to this world (and imagine that the technicians of Baikanur and Cape Kennedy, the agricultural engineers in the experimental farmlands of Africa and South America, were treated as indisputably holy men; imagine some bookworm asking Bénezet his opinion on, for example, Petrus Lombardus's view of the humanity of Christ, and receiving the answer: "Look, buddy, hold that lever tight—that goddamn stone's still not sitting right.") In 1216, the old count Raymond VI of Toulouse and his son are given a festive welcome into the town. Ten years later (a year after the birth of Thomas Aquinas), Avignon refuses to grant free passage to the cruel King Louis the Lion, who is advancing against the count of Toulouse and the Albigensians; after a siege of three months the town is forced to capitulate, and then watch regretfully as, a few days later, too late, the campsite of the besieging army is flooded by the Durance. In 1229, the county of Venaissin—to which Carpentras, Cavaillon, Vaison, and Pernes, but not yet Avignon, belong—is given to the pope by Raymond VII of Toulouse. It must have been at about that time (while in Flanders Sister Hadewych is discoursing on Love with Sara, Emma, and Margriet) that the *cours d'amour* are established: in Signe and Pierrefeu judgments are reportedly handed down by, for instance, Adalarie, Viscountess of Avignon, Mabille, Dame of Hyères, and Countess of Dye; in Avignon by, for example, Jehanne, Dame of Baulx, Huguette of Forcalquier, Mabille de Villeneuve, Dame of Vence, and Blanche of Flassans, nicknamed Blankaflour. (In 1260, the first flagellants appear in Italy, Meister Eckhart is born not far from Gotha in Hochheim, Thuringia, and—fourteen years later—Thomas Aquinas dies.) At that time Avignon has between five and six thousand inhabitants, about as many as Dinant or Medemblik, Uzès, Tarascon, or Saint-Rémy. (Between 1284 and 1304—thus, in the space of some twenty years—the following are born: Simone Martini, Ruysbroeck, Suso, Ockham, Tauler, Bridget of Sweden, and Petrarch. A year after Petrarch's death, the Gascon Bertrand de Got, Archbishop of Bordeaux, is elected pope and crowned at Lyon under the name Clement V; a year after the birth of Laura de Noves in Avignon, he moves into the Dominican monastery, where he probably prepared the forthcoming Council. The Council meets in Vienne and decides to abolish the order of the Knights Templar; the main beneficiaries of the forfeited goods will be the Knights

Hospitaller of St. John, who have fled to Rhodes (and in Flanders we have a legend that Willem van Saeftinghe joined them); the condemnation of the Beguines and their male counterparts the Beghards may be nothing more than a healthy reaction against degenerate spiritualism, but in the ruling against the vow of poverty and against the followers of Olier, it's difficult to see anything other than a Byzantine distinction between a Platonic acceptance of evangelical poverty and the hard and painful reality of it. After the Council, the Pope moves into the castle of Monteux near Carpentras, the capital of the papal domain and a sanctuary for Jews; in 1314 he falls seriously ill, and sets out on a journey to his native region, but scarcely has he crossed the Rhone at Roquemaure—before the Curia has even left Carpentras—than he dies. The conclave that meets in Carpentras has to be adjourned because of the machinations and threats of the Gascons: the cardinals flee to Avignon, and not until 1316 do they finally meet in Lyon. Cardinal Jacques Duèse or Deuse or d'Euse is elected, the elderly but very fit former Bishop of Avignon—who consequently, quite naturally, settles in his former episcopal seat—as John XXII. Is it unjust to see him as a kind of brilliant notary? By preferring his own countrymen from Quercy, he's acting no differently than his predecessor did toward the Gascons, and by relying on the support of the Guelphs in Italy—the city of Florence, the King of Sicily, and Robert of Anjou, the Count of Provence—he does no more than use the most obvious means to avert an awkward political situation; but the centralization of all benefices, which he is able to push through with Gasbert de Laval, seems mainly the work of an intelligent bureaucrat. (Fifty years later, when Urban V returns to Rome, the papal administration will have expanded into a dizzying apparatus, scarcely transportable any longer.) So how can one resist the temptation to attribute both the bull "Gloriosam Ecclesiam," against the Fraticelli, and (five years later, a year after the recruitment of Paolo of Siena, the year when the *Chapelle Saint-Etienne* is decorated by Pierre Dupuy, "frère mineur de Toulouse") the canonization of Thomas Aquinas, that expert bookkeeper of salvation, as well as (another four years later—the year that Laura de Sade is first seen by Petrarch) the condemnation of Marsilius of Padua, who in *Defensor pacis* had advocated the division of church and state, and (two years later still) that against the heresies of Meister Eckhart, to this same bourgeois, probably well-meaning, possessive mentality? (By that time, of course, Eckhart is already dead, but a certain little boy, who is probably not yet called Wycliffe, is five years old.) It's not only the *fratres minores*, the mystics and the professors of absolute poverty who are a thorn in Jacques Duèse's side. He himself is accused of heresy by the excommunicated Ludwig of Bavaria—another advocate of the division of church and state, and one who can in addition appeal to Eckhart for support, and in 1321 appoint the Franciscan Pietro da Corvara as Antipope. If only another crusade could be organized, then Christians would go back to paying more attention to the heathen than to the divine qualities of the preconditions for salvation; but because of the conflict between the English and French kings, the dispatch of a squadron has no effect. The following year, Pietro da Corvara withdraws, but a year later, on All Hallows, John preaches the blessedness of the souls separated from the body by death: was this bravado? or did he really think he could convince the faithful? What it boils down to is that this pope can't understand how the salvation of the deceased can be complete when they are separated from their fellow living beings—so earthly, so social, so focused on the here and now is this notary's concept of the soul. But for the vast majority of ordinary believers this view is unacceptable: for their daily misery on earth they demand immediate, complete recompense after their last gasp—what else could this faith be good for, that the wretched of the world had already renounced so much to embrace, unless it offered a miraculous, blazing return on their investment? . . . *and they screamed at him. All Europe screamed: this was a bad belief.* He has to recant, John XXII, and the following day he dies. (Perhaps he prefers not to outlive the abandonment of his now desecrated belief? or is the recantation the work of cardinals who feel as little pity for a dying heretic as for a living one, even if he is pope? though, God knows, the heretic may yet discover immediately after his death that he was right after all?) His elected successor is the pious, unimpeachable theologian Jacques Fournier, a Cistercian monk active in fighting the Albigensians who takes the name Benedict XII. He is not a lawyer, and to everyone's surprise it won't be possible to accuse him of nepotism (inasmuch as anyone was looking to do so). Unlike his predecessor, who thought very seriously, if not of returning directly to Rome, then of moving provisionally to Bologna, Benedict installs himself in Avignon and has the episcopal palace rebuilt for the purpose. In order to compensate somewhat for the rather idiosyncratic ideas of Jacques Duèse, an edict is issued on the fate of man after death. Five years after being elected pope—and there can be no doubt that the enmity between the English and French kings justifies the presence of the pope in Avignon—the Hundred Years' War breaks out. That same year, Simone Martini arrives in Avignon together with his wife and brother; he paints the tympanum of the porch of *Notre-Dame des Doms* and his pupils decorate the vestibule of what is turning into the palace; he has regular meetings with Petrarch, illuminates the title page of his *Codice di Virgilio*, and in 1342 paints the panel of the Holy Family after the dispute with the Pharisees, his last known work. That same year, Benedict XII dies, and is succeeded by the French Benedictine Pierre Roger: Clement VI. The disastrous bankruptcies of the Florentine merchant houses obviously do not prevent him from acting as patron, particularly to Matteo Giovanetti of Viterbo, the technician of the fresco, and the members of his studio: Riccone and Giovanni of Arezzo, Pietro of Viterbo, Francesco and Nicole from Florence, Giovanni of Lucca. In addition, a crusade is initiated, but the initial victory at Smyrna—again because of the war between the French and English—is not exploited. Simone dies that year. (Three years later a girl is born who will be called Catherine of Siena, and the following year the Black Death breaks out in Europe. The *Mur de la Peste* near Fontaine-de-Vaucluse must have been built at about this time, to prevent the sick from entering the Comtat? Pope Clement begins the building of the second, real papal palace, buys the entire town for eight thousand guilders from Johanna of Naples, and establishes a mint. That year sees the death of Laura de Sade—of the plague? The year 1350 is declared a Jubilee year, and so anyone who undertakes a pilgrimage to Rome receives a full indulgence; probably the Pope hopes in this way to compensate somewhat for his absence from the Holy City, where the impatient and quick-tongued Birgitta of Sweden awaits his arrival, but it's hardly far-fetched to suggest that these pilgrimages contribute to the spread of the Black Death. In 1352, the Pope dies in Avignon, and is succeeded by the old, sick Grand Penitentiary Etienne Aubert, considered innocuous by the other cardinals, who chooses the name of Innocent. But no sooner has he been declared pope than he annuls the compromise adopted by the members of the conclave for the selection of a pope, under which the authority of every pope from that point on would be subordinate to that of the College of Cardinals—obviously the obduracy, brilliance, or liberalism of the last few popes was considered far too dangerous. Innocent VI entrusts all papal interests in Italy to the strategist Cardinal Albornoz, and in 1356 he founds the *Chartreuse du Val-de-Bénédiction* at Villeneuve. But then Avignon is threatened by marauding bands of freebooters, the *grandes compagnies*, unleashed by truces in the Anglo-French wars, and so the building of the third, crenellated town wall must be begun. Pope Innocent dies in 1362, waiting for King John the

Good, with whose help he hoped to undertake a crusade. The pious, peace-loving, scholarly Guillaume de Grimoard, abbot of the *Abbaye Saint-Victor* at Marseille, succeeds him as Urban V. For the benefit of students, he founds a college at Montpellier, and in Avignon he sets up a library and a courtyard garden now called the orchard of Urban V. He actively promotes a crusade under Peter of Cyprus, but the chivalry-minded John the Good dies and his successor Charles the Wise has completely different priorities. In 1365, heresies are again condemned "on the state of perfection and on poverty." The following year (the year of Suso's death) the negotiations with the Patriarch of Constantinople, John V Palaeologus, go well, but the Pope's presence in his papal seat becomes necessary as a result, all the more so since Rome no longer seems so hazardous. In 1367—six hundred years before these words are written—the pope of whom one would have least expected it forces himself to leave Avignon—his library, his peaceful courtyard garden—for Marseille, embarking from there for Rome. (And this is only possible for him because he is leaving behind the greater part of his financial and administrative apparatus.) In 1369 (the year in which Johannes Hus is born), Palaeologus submits to the Pope's authority, but then war breaks out again, now between Edward III and Charles the Wise, and—convinced that he will be better able to mediate from Avignon (and perhaps in some small part because of his books?)—the Pope, despite the admonitions of Queen Birgitta, returns to the north. In that year, the argument that Christ through his death had actually betrayed everything he worked for is condemned (an argument that now, six hundred years later, is postulated by Anglo-Saxon theologians). Urban soon dies, and his successor Gregory XI, Pierre Roger de Beaufort—a nephew of Pierre Roger, who had become Clement VI—realizes that (because of the building of the palace? of the town wall? because of the payments to all the well-known and then less well-known painters? because of the cost of the library? of traveling?) he simply doesn't have sufficient funds to return to Rome. His legates succeed in starting negotiations between Charles V and Edward III, in Calais and later in Bruges, and they reach a truce. (Petrarch dies, and Birgitta of Sweden dies, but her father-confessor joins Catherine of Siena.) In Italy, Guelph church provinces rebel against the Pope, who imposes an interdict and instructs the legate Robert of Geneva—prince and cardinal, son of the count of Geneva and the countess of Boulogne—to take harsh measures. Catherine of Siena herself comes to Avignon to beg the Pope to return to Rome, and the following year Gregory undertakes the journey. At this time Avignon has some thirty thousand inhabitants, about as many as Lokeren or Sittard, Arles or Albi today, as many as Bruges at the time and fewer only than Paris and the largest Italian towns. (In Rome, the theses of Wycliffe are denounced. When Gregory dies the following year, the great, ludicrous confusion begins: the cardinals elect Bartolomeo Prignano, who is not a member of the College of Cardinals, but until he announces his acceptance and out of fear of the turbulent populace of Rome, they use the disguised Cardinal Tebaldeschi as a double. Bartolomeo accepts the papacy, chooses the name Urban, and then starts behaving with such extraordinary severity that the French cardinals go to Fondi, where they declare the choice of pope invalid and elect the merciless Robert of Geneva as Pope Clement VI. Urban is recognized in England, Flanders, Poland, Hungary, Germany and Italy; Clement in France, Sicily, Scotland, Castile, Aragon and Navarre, Portugal, Savoy and on Cyprus. When he does not succeed in establishing himself in Rome, Clement moves to Avignon where he has immediate access to the papal finances. Paradoxically, the court of the accursed antipope is given a certain luster by the saintly figure of young Pierre de Luxembourg, who became a cardinal at fifteen. (Within eight years the following people die: Ruysbroeck (in Groenendaal, in the woods of Brabant), Catherine of Siena, Wycliffe, and also Pierre de Luxembourg, at whose grave miraculous things happen. When Urban VI dies in Rome, he is succeeded by Boniface IX). In 1394 (in Flanders the Clementine clergy are boycotted, and the only people on whom Philip the Bold does not impose the Avignon pope are the inhabitants of Ghent), Clement VII dies, and the members of the Avignon conclave all take an oath to do everything in their power to heal the schism and if need be to withdraw if any of them are elected pope. So whatever got into the Aragonese Pedro de Luna immediately after his election as Benedict XIII? He cannot, may not, does not even want to think of stepping down, and it seems that suddenly and inexplicably he felt wholly invested with the formidable, compelling *plenitudo potestatis*. And what role does his father-confessor, Vincent

Ferrier play in this decision? But meanwhile he is another anti-pope who can boast the friendship of a man in whom the whole Church will later recognize a saint. But then Benedict loses the obedience of France—that is, France, Sicily, Castile, Navarre, and Provence—and at a stroke his principal source of income. Unsurprisingly he is deserted by all the cardinals except five—even by the keeper of the seal, and thus likewise by his seal. Because of him Avignon is besieged by the renegade Geoffroi de Boucicaut; when this rather inconvenient siege is lifted—because the town resists all too effectively?—Benedict XIII is assigned Avignon as his compulsory residence. But after four years the indefatigable antipope manages to escape from Avignon in disguise, and for ages wanders through Provence, Languedoc, and Roussillon. (In Rome Boniface IX is succeeded by Innocent VII, and the latter by Gregory XII. The Council of Pisa—which also excommunicates Johannes Hus—tries to end the schism by electing a third pope: Alexander V. After his death—in the year that Enguerrand Charonton dies, some where near Laon—he is succeeded by the antipope John XXIII.) At the Council of Constance (where the heresies of Wycliffe are indicted, and where Johannes Hus, although granted safe conduct by Emperor Sigismund on leaving Prague, is treacherously burned alive as a heretic; *o sancta simplicitas* he cries, when he sees an old woman dragging a few fagots to the stake (but for all we know it was out of sympathy with the woman, since the fiercer the fire the shorter the agony?)), Gregory is prevailed upon to relinquish the papacy, but the unyielding Benedict XIII is deposed instead.

(Finally John XXIII is also deposed, and Martin V is elected in Rome.) Not until two years later does Pedro de Luna die, aged ninety-four, disowned by the whole of Christianity but still pope, on the Spanish peninsula of Peñiscola, some two hundred kilometers south of Barcelona. Henceforth there will be only a legate or vice-legate in Avignon. But as if to compensate for the absence of the popes, it is now painters who settle in and around Avignon. In about 1425 a certain Nicolas Froment is born in Uzès. Twenty years later the panel of the *Aix Annunciation* is painted—perhaps by the mysterious Jean Chapus, suspected of heresy and even Satanism, who must have been familiar both with the work of Van Eyck and with that of Konrad Witz and Claus Sluter of the Dijon School. Two years later Enguerrand Charonton moves to Avignon, staying first in the *Place Saint-Pierre*, and afterwards in the *Rue de la Saunerie*. (In Aix, Netherlanders like Bartholomeus de Clerc and Coppin Delf work for the "Roi René.") In 1460, someone paints the *Pietà of Villeneuve*; Charonton dies six years later, but shortly afterward Nicolas Froment arrives in Avignon, where he will reside in the *Place du Puits-aux-Boeufs*. Eight years later he paints the *Burning Bush* triptych, decorates the livery—that is, the *hôtel*—of Viviers in the *Rue Hercule*, and seven years after that (in the year of Luther's birth), he dies. This is when the present façade of the *Eglise Saint-Agricol* is built, along with the *Hôtel de Baroncelli-Javon*, now called *Palais du Roure*. So does nothing else happen in Avignon in the next eighty years? (Monteverdi was born in Cremona, a Council met at Trent, the Jesuit order was founded, and in the Low Countries it's the time of Grotius, Rembrandt, Vondel, and Rubens.) Was Nostradamus in Avignon in 1575? The façade of the *Hôtel des Monnaies* was built in 1619, the *Chapelle de la Visitation* in 1632, and meanwhile the *Pont Saint-Bénezet* collapsed (after having been in use for some four hundred and fifty years). It is in 1644 that an English traveler, namely John Evelyn, stops at Avignon on his way to Rome: *The City is plac'd on the Rhodanus, and divided from the newer part, or Towne (which is situated on the other side of the River) by a very fair bridge of stone, which has been broken, at one of whose ex-treames is a very high rock on which a strong Castle well furnish'd with Artillery. The Walls of the City (being all square huge free stone) are absolutely the most neate and best in repaire that in my life I ever saw: it is full of well built Palaces: Those of the Vice Legats & Archbish: being the most magnificent: Many sumptuous Churches, especially that of St. Magdalene & St. Martial, wherein the Card: d'Amboise is the most observable: That of the Celestines where Clement the 8th* (sic) *lies buried, the Altar whereof is ex-ceeding rich; but for nothing I more admir'd it than the Tomb of Madona Laura Petrarchs celebrated Mistris.* From about 1650 on, Avignon Carmelites embroider the vestments which more than three centuries later will be exhibited in the *Chapelle de l'Oratoire.* A century or so later the *Hôtel de Villeneuve-Martignan* is built, which will later become the *Musée Calvet.* In Saumane lives a noble toddler called Alphonse Donatien de Sade, in 1763 he is twenty-three and until a few days before his marriage to Renée-Pélagie Cordier de Launay continues an affair with an unknown girl from Avignon; three years later he is again in Avignon, together with his uncle Abbé d'Ebbreuil, and for the next ten years he will live mainly in La Coste. In 1790 or 1791 Avignon is annexed by France—which is actually not yet a republic. It must be some thirty years after Sade's death that Mérimée, passing through Avignon, arranges for Enguerrand Charonton's *Couronnement de la Vierge* to be taken to the hospice of Villeneuve for safety; he writes: *Avignon is filled with churches and palaces, all provided with battlemented and machicolated towers. The Palace of the Pope is a model of a fortification for the Middle Ages, which proves what amiable security reigned toward the fourteenth century . . . The natives are as proud of their Inquisition as the English of their Magna Charta. "We also," say they, "have had autos-da-fé, and the Spaniards had none until after us!"* Three years later a theatre is built and later the *Hôtel de Ville*. In October 1867, Étienne Mallarmé, a teacher of English, along with his wife and young daughter, moves into number 8 *Place Portail Matheron.* Jens Peter Jacobsen must have spent time in Avignon in 1873 or 1876: *In the graceful pleasure-gardens behind the Pope's ancient palace in Avignon stands a bench from which one can overlook the Rhone, the flowery banks of the Durance, hills and fields, and a part of the town.* (And an improbable alternative translation reads: *The view of the rich banks of the Rhone is splendid from the gardens surrounding the old papal palace in Avignon.*) Rainer Maria Rilke arrives some thirty-five years later: *From the other bank of the Rhone, seen from Villeneuve, the city, God knows why, made me think of Novgorod, the great . . .* Seventeen years later he dies in Sierre, much further up the same valley. In 1926 there are forty-eight thousand inhabitants in the city on the Rhone, that is, as many as there are now in Périgueux, Den Helder, or Aalst, and twenty-five thousand less than at the moment when *he* first arrives in Avignon.

Those are the facts. Are they the full facts? No, not all, one can't know them all, one can't even know the facts he knows, and certainly not list them. One can, though, list the books in his library that he used in compiling his chronology: J. Dupont and Cesare Gnud, *La peinture Gothique* (Geneva, 1954); J. Lassaigne and G. C. Argan, *De Van Eyck à Botticelli* (Geneva, 1955); Jacques de Voragine, *La Légende Dorée* (Paris, 1956); R. M. Rilke, *The Notebooks of Malte Laurids Brigge* (Wiesbaden, 1951); P. Mérimée. *Letters to an Incognita* I (Paris, 1874); J. P. Jacobsen, *Mogens and other Stories* (Copenhagen, 1882); Rilke, *Letters* (Wiesbaden, 1950); Belgian Railways, *Official Travel Guide* (Tournai, 1966); *The Diary of John Evelyn* (London, 1959); Denzinger-Schömetzer, *Enchiridion Symbolorum, Definitionum et Declarationum de rebus fidei et morum* (Barcelona, 1963); Y. Renouard, *The Avignon Papacy* (Paris, 1954); Zoé Oldenbourg, *Massacre at Montsegur* (Paris, 1959); J. Lafitte-Houssat, *Troubadours et Cours d'Amour* (Paris, 1950); M. Pobé & J.Rast, *Provence* (Olten/Freiburg i.B., 1962); Evelyn Sandberg-Vavalà, *Simone Martini* (Milan, 1956); Sade, *Oeuvres* (Paris, 1961).

One can also write (this emerges from allusions by Jacqueline, and also from certain books of Georges Simenon's) that

Avignon is, or was, a stopping-off place on the *remonte*, the route north taken by prostitutes recruited in the south.

One can also write: He still doesn't know what the painting *Les demoiselles d'Avignon* really has to do with the town.

One can also write (as is clear from a letter sent to him on October 11, 1958 by Rose Escoffier: *Here the Rhone has swollen above danger level, but because of* (sic) *the special pumps which have been used to prevent the flooding of the lower town, it flooded only the* allées de l'Oulle *and the* île de la Barthelasse (*an island between that arm of the living Rhone and the dead Rhone on the other side*) that there are pumping stations that prevent the lower town—the western section that borders the *Boulevard de l'Oulle?* or the northern section east of the Promenade?—from flooding, and also that between Avignon and Villeneuve there are two kinds of Rhone, the living and the dead.

One can also write: In Avignon in the northeast on the *Rue Carréterie*, in the southwest on the *Rue Velouterie*, in the northwest on the *Rue Plaisance*, and in the southwest on the *Rue Séverine*, there are thoroughfares he most probably has never been down.

One can also write: When he thinks of Avignon, the concrete, sharp, unforgettably objective images that are invoked in him are surprisingly and embarrassingly rare; for example, though he sees plane trees in the *Rue de la République*, and also the large, smooth, oblong paving slabs (the same as you could find—until recently?—on the Louizalaan in Brussels, the same as on various Paris boulevards); but he could not say how the pavement is laid around the tree trunks, for example, whether just a ring or rectangle of bare earth has been left around the base of the tree or whether that earth, as it almost always is in Paris, is protected by a cast-iron grille (why? cigarette butts and scraps of paper are still thrown or pushed through the grille . . .); and he would, for example, answer unhesitatingly in the negative if he was asked whether the streets of Avignon have cable strung above them, but this answer would be more the result of a disguised rationalization (there are no trolleys in Avignon, and there can't possibly be that many power lines for streetlights on the busier streets, because, for example, there are so many tree branches in the way, and in the less populous streets there simply isn't very much lighting at all) than an image in his memory (and there are plenty of other explanations for this unreliable impression: the fact that the cables are simply hidden by foliage in summer, and in winter are engulfed entirely by the dazzling lights; besides which the fact that any inhabitant of Brussels, where in many places one feels he's walking under a gigantic spiderweb, is bound to feel relieved in Avignon). His memory is like a bas-relief in silver or copper in which the greater part of the surface has been oxidized and darkened by time, with only here and there—usually on the characters in the foreground, but sometimes also in the most insignificant places—sections, little ones, invariably, that he has apparently been polishing, unthinkingly as the lenses of his glasses. Such an observation leads to humility: after all, he still believes that one is only alive for the principal purpose of observing the objects in the world.

One can also write: or should one perhaps accept that Avignon is inexpressible?

One can also write: He sometimes feels that proper names betray the existence of a secret second life, an underground network of which only sporadic outcrops are visible to him. Not primarily in the frequency with which he finds himself mentioning the same names over and again—Mistral, Villeneuve, Vachères, Vaison—with disparate meanings or in different contexts, because that could if necessary be explained historically, geographically, or simply by chance. But that the name of one of the gates of Avignon should be the same as that of the cleaner and washerwoman who worked for him during his stays in the village, and who resembled Breughel's Dulle Griet, and the same too as that of the last eastern pass over the Lubéron, the *Col de la Mort d'Imbert*, about eight kilometers from the same village; that the house he moved into in the village was the one that had once been—when? and why?—the *Hôtel de Baroncelli-Javon*; that the name of the street where he found the blonde girl in Avignon was the same as that of the Brussels avenue where, two years earlier, he had first professed to her something extraordinarily like what is commonly called love; that the name of the village of Noves had to serve twice over—the first time through an excavated sculpture linked to a religious legend, the second time through a marriage and a blood relationship—as a mysterious link between the virtuous, indomitable beauty of a woman and a frightening, gruesome, violent scene: such facts arouse suspicion.

One can also write: He never entered the *Palais des Papes*. The reasons he gives, spontaneously, to explain this omission—that he always lacked the time, felt too tired or languid or lazy to undertake the lengthy visit, which he had heard his mother, perhaps the very first time he passed through Avignon, call particularly tiring; or else that something like a conceited, arrogant inertia prevented him from lining up with all the tourists at the entrance gate—are not terribly convincing: anyone who stops at Avignon is quite simply obliged, like Mérimée or Rilke or any other tourist, to visit the *Palais des Papes*. But the fact is that he doesn't regret his lack of curiosity, or his laziness, or his hesitancy. Because isn't it better not to enter such a building at all than to enter it in a way (Rilke needed seventeen days) that one feels, subsequently, was shamefully inadequate? Because, after all, can't this secret space now be all the better illuminated by his imagination? Because, after all, as long as he hasn't yet entered the palace, and as long as he still has a valid reason for going to the town, he can believe that he has not yet forfeited all chance of knowing Avignon exhaustively? And one can write: In Avignon, between the *Promenade du Rocher des Doms* and a tangle of ancient alleyways, there is a very large building. *September 10, 1843 . . . In the Palace of the Popes you ascend a hundred steps of a winding stairway and then find yourself suddenly facing a wall. Turning your head, you see, fifteen feet above you, the continuation of the stairway, which can only be reached by means of a ladder. There are, also, subterranean chambers, which were used during the Inquisition. You are*

shown furnaces where the irons were heated to torture the her-
etics, and the remains of a complicated instrument, also used for
torture . . . —With prayers and curses, blessings and anathemas
ringing in our ears we follow the guide, who recites the text that
has been drummed into him, through the labyrinth of branching
wings of the double palace, which despite its unequal construc-
tion gives the impression, because of its great weight and mass,
of being all of a piece, across echoing courtyards to rooms the size
of churches, through magnificently painted galleries, up staircases
that seem to have been dug by moles into the thick wall, into kitch-
ens whose hearths have room for a whole ox, stopping briefly at
dizzyingly high windows and on terraces from where one's gaze
descends onto the gray muddle of streets and squares, and finally
down again via a last staircase to the courtyard, which alarms us
with its gigantic proportions. One can write: In Avignon then,
next to the church where a pope once ruthlessly professed his
belief in human solidarity beyond death, stands the great edifice
built by Benedict XII and especially Clement VI, where Innocent VI lived, and which Urban V and Gregory XI—and later
too, in secret, like a thief, Benedict XII, whose holy obstinacy
is quite disturbing—left with finality . . . as if this building were
less a residence than a point of departure for the Eternal City or
the hereafter. A borehole in time by means of which it should be
possible, as with the annual rings of a felled tree, to see back to
the period when a pope could be charged with heresy. A core, a
stone, a mystical castle of the soul, a Kaaba to which he might
be forever denied entry.

One can also write (he forgets from which newspaper and when he must have learned this): In Avignon or in Villeneuve, on the right bank, bodies are occasionally washed up, and there is usually talk of the gangster who controls the *remonte*.

One can also write: He wonders whether there was ever a *Rue des Ursulines* in Avignon; whether there was never an Ursuline convent in the town.

One can also write: It turns out (turns out because he leafed through what travel guide?) that the most heavily used town gate, the *Porte de la République*—formed by the gap, opposite the station, between two pavilions, the left-hand one occupied by an *Essi* office, where he occasionally went to book a taxi to the village, and which in summer fly flags—was only built in the nineteenth century.

One can also write (as is made clear in a newspaper article he comes across by chance): Since 1947 there has been an annual festival in Avignon, initially devoted to theater, with performances by Jean Vilar's TNP company, but now also to ballet, music, and film; in 1967 use was made of the *Cours d'honneur* in the Palace, as well as the *Cloître des Carmes* and the *Verger d'Urbain V*; obviously this festival is the pretext for putting out all those flags during the summer.

One can also write: Jacqueline maintained, in a childishly mysterious tone, that an unusually large number of Avignon children are born with deformities, and that this is the fault of radioactive materials carried by the mistral from nuclear power plants—Pierrelatte? or Marcoule?

One can also write: He has forgotten in which book or magazine he found an allusion to the celebrated and revolutionary regulations supposedly drawn up by Joan of Naples for the whores of Avignon.

One can also write: He finds it strange that he should immerse himself to such a degree in Avignon, when not Avignon but nearby Aix is the town where he would most like to live.

One can also write: In Avignon there is a house.

One can also write: In Avignon a window on one floor was lit all night long.

One can also write (but the more words one writes down the greater the precision of the assertion, the greater the number of possibilities excluded, the greater the chance of one's being wrong, the smaller the probability that what has been written tallies with some reality): In Avignon a woman once kept watch all night in the room of a sick child.

One can also write (writing is stating explicitly is making experience culminate in words is praising is glorifying): In Avignon there are lovers who make love.

One can also write: One day a man will arrive in Avignon.

One day a man will arrive, and satisfactorily; one day someone must ultimately arrive in Avignon. Not by car on the *nationale sept*, or on the other side of the town over the *Pont Saint-Pierre* and through the *Porte de l'Oulle*, or along the *Route de Marseille* and the *Porte l'Imbert*: caution demands that he rely on the railway used for so many arrivals over the last hundred years; perhaps he also prefers it because, unlike the three motorways that head straight for the city center and split the town in two, the train from the north encloses it in an elegant, engaging, almost caressing curve, so that the traveler getting off the train can imagine that his arrival has left the town intact, but that nevertheless it cannot escape him, held firmly as it is by the pincer movement of the train between the railway and the river. What train will he arrive on (since words make, demand, oblige)? A night train is tempting, but in that case, unless the present timetable were radically changed, he would arrive from Paris at the earliest at about four in the morning, at the latest at about six-thirty; and then it would be doubtful whether, even if he had booked a couchette, with the excitement that inevitably accompanies every journey, and after a trip of seven hours or more, if he left from somewhere farther away than Paris, and because of the slight, never completely suppressed fear of missing his stop, he would be awake enough upon arrival to observe nocturnal or early-morning Avignon to full effect from the word go. So would it be better to take *Le Mistral* which leaves the *Gare de Lyon* at one in the afternoon and gets into Avignon at thirteen minutes past seven in the evening? But then he wouldn't be able to have supper on the train, and together with worrying about his luggage, and, even though a room has been booked, about the hotel where he is to spend the night, his hunger threatens to divert attention from his arrival, his decisive arrival. So, after all, the best solution seems to be to take the morning train at a quarter to eight or a quarter past nine, getting in at two-seventeen or four-eleven, on which he can have both breakfast and lunch. He would be well advised to spend the duration of the journey in relative inactivity, or at least not to get involved in any exciting conversations or in reading a fascinating novel or thriller; the ideal way to kill time would be by reading a daily or weekly or flicking through some particularly knotty academic work (for example, on *La fiscalité pontificale en France au XIVe-siècle*), smoking a cigarette or a pipe in the corridor, maybe a visit to the bar, if there is one: after all, a certain boredom, as long as it does not have a stultifying effect, can only benefit one's concentration. For the sake of keeping that concentration intact, he would also be well advised to book his hotel room before leaving the *Gare de Lyon*. The question of which hotel immediately arises: he has an ample choice in town, from the pinched, already familiar *Hôtel du Centre* to the expensive, four-star *Hôtel de l'Europe* almost opposite the *Pont Saint-Pierre*, behind the *Porte de l'Oulle*—only the noisy, characterless kind of transit hotel like *Paris-Nice* ought to be excluded; but perhaps it would be even better if he were to acknowledge right away the special character of Avignon by staying out of town at first, for example in Villeneuve; if staying there proved inconvenient, or later, when he was sufficiently familiar with the exterior of the town, then he would enter the walls. And then, there's also the question of what time of year he's chosen for this journey. So that his arrival should be as tranquil as possible, the turbulent summertime—when the merciless blue of the sky is obscured by the dense foliage of the plane trees, as if the density of the foliage and that of the tourist population were always in direct proportion, and when it's impossible to see anything but the kaleidoscopic teeming of the lightly, colorfully dressed vacationers—should be ruled out; but because that summer rush is also definitely part of Avignon—indeed, is the only image of Avignon that a far from negligible number of people retain—and because it is difficult to predict with certainty whether his stay will last twelve or nine months, his arrival should ideally be scheduled for spring, if possible; and to avoid his immediately being distracted by the euphoria of the Provençal springtime, should in fact occur at the end of winter.

Just over an hour after the stop in Valence, when Montélimar, Orange, Bédarrides, and Sorgues have slid by in succession, probably unrecognized, the train will brush the Rhone for the last time; when it quite suddenly turns south, away from the bank, it will be time to retrieve one's suitcase from the luggage rack, put on one's coat, and—from the corridor, if it's on the side of the right-hand track as well as the river—to take a first look at the town one is to visit. It would be just as well to bear in mind that the train passes in succession over the *Route du Pontet* (where the *nationale sept* and the *nationale cent* merge), over the *Chemin du Cimetière*, and shortly afterward over a street or road the name of which is not given on the map; then over the *Chemin Saint-Jean* (which leads to the *Porte Thiers*), the *Route de Montfavet*, and the *Route de Marseille* which leads to the *Porte l'Imbert*), after the *Chemin de la*

Trillade, des Sources (which leads to the *Boulevard Gabriel Péri* opposite the *Portail Magnanen*), and *de l'Arrousaire*, over the *Boulevard Saint-Ruf* (leading to the *Porte Saint-Michel*), and then, finally, a hundred meters or so before the station, over the *Avenue Monclar*; because from nowhere else will he be able to see these streets as he sees them from the train. Then the train will stop, he will get off, probably follow not too large a number of passengers into the dirty, malodorous passage that leads from the first and second tracks to the platform. A man arrives in Avignon. Lining up at the ticket collector's booth he will probably be able to look at the few people who, necks craned, are waiting for some other arriving passenger, and think that it would not be unpleasant to find oneself waited for (and then, here, he dispenses with the tempting romantic possibility that he is being waited for unexpectedly by a woman he doesn't even know); as he hands over his ticket he may recognize a first southern accent. As soon as he got off the train, or maybe even before, he will have seen whether the weather permits a walk. When he turns left to the baggage check to leave his suitcase, the frosted glass panels will probably prevent him from looking toward the town. Turning around, he won't go to the exit yet, but to the *salle des pas perdus* to note down the arrival and departure times of the buses to Villeneuve; if no timetable is visible, they'll probably be able to help him at the information office at the other side of the booking hall. Only then will he go outside. On the terrace past the entrance he'll stop and look. In the foreground a few buses, a line of taxis along the pavement of the roads describing a circle around the public garden that touches the station building; people leaving, arriving, with and without suitcases; bushes, trees—plane trees already? certainly there are further on, beyond the *Porte de la République*; loiterers, idlers, including some North Africans, waiting for God knows what; in the background the intersection and its traffic lights, on the station side two wooden, pavilion-like cafés, across the street, built from the same stone as the walls, the two *Essi* pavilions; no flags yet; higher up: the sky, perhaps overcast, but possibly as clear as it only ever is here. Once he's looked his fill at the very mundane surroundings of the station, only coincidentally rendered archetypal or picturesque—by the seemingly bewildered presence of a farming couple, for instance, or by the noisy joviality of a few natives—he will set out very slowly, as cautiously as a recovering patient. (If it's raining he'll be able to wait by the entrance until it clears up again, or venture out on his walk anyway, if it is not raining too heavily or if he's come equipped with an umbrella.) Not to Villeneuve yet, and not to the town center either: after two cafés he will turn—right or left?—onto the *Boulevard Estienne d'Orves*. (Sooner or later words force one into a choice, a narrowing down, at some point the lustrous density of all the unexpressed possibilities must be attacked, pulverized, melted down, dissolved.) A glance at the map offers reasons, or pretexts, for turning left: by proceeding in a clockwise direction on this first tour of the town, he will not retrace his own steps after returning to the station in order to take a bus or a taxi to the Pont Saint-Pierre; this direction too has the advantage of putting the sun at his back if he were to follow the boulevards *Saint-Dominique, du Rhône, de la Ligne* and *Saint-Lazare* along the Rhone, which might not be tree-lined. This walk around the town walls will take at least an hour, hopefully longer, and naturally he will make use of favorably appointed cafés to rest, drink, relieve himself, or simply quietly absorb the walls and life—or the absence of life—around them. It would be best if he had not a thick, cumbersome guidebook with him, but simply a map, so that whenever he wants he can identify a building or determine his location. When he gets back to the *Porte de la République*, he will collect his case from the station and take a taxi or a bus to the right bank of the Rhone.

Then it becomes increasingly difficult to put the course of this ultimate arrival into words. The possibility has already been tacitly excluded not only that Avignon might be wiped off the map, or become inaccessible by train, or that the train might be somehow disabled, or that bad weather might make his walk around the town completely impossible (so that he would be obliged to postpone this circuit, or if need be replace it with a slow taxi ride), or that the baggage check office might be closed, but also that he might find himself simply unable, no matter how he tries, to force himself to enter the town center that afternoon—instead leaving Avignon by the first train or drowning himself in the Rhone. The very prediction of his arrival has led, as it were behind the scenes, to his acquiring not only a suitcase (as if it was inconceivable that he should travel without luggage?) but also an overcoat or a raincoat, an umbrella, a map, and money to pay the bill in one or more cafés, as well as for accommodation in a hotel. In Villeneuve he won't be able to escape the influence of a hotel manager, male or female, hotel staff, other guests—people who are far less reliable than stone walls, boulevards, trains, or even ticket collectors or taxi and bus drivers. The preservation of a sense of verisimilitude and moreover of his ability to find a beneficial use, in terms of his reconnaissance, for any of the unexpected discoveries and phenomena he might stumble over in Avignon—or which the town itself might fling in his direction—require that his behavior following these initial movements through the city be determined only very loosely. But his entry into the town is already too momentous to be left to chance or improvisation. And the very existence of twelve town gates means that he would need to have used them all before one could speak of a truly ultimate entry; a particular plan of attack must be devised: the first day, for example, he might enter, for example, the *Porte de la Ligne* at one in the afternoon, and exit by the *Porte de la République*; the second day, enter the town at two o'clock through the *Porte Saint-Lazare* and not leave until eight o'clock by the *Porte Saint-Charles*; spend the third day in town from three o'clock until nine o'clock, entering through the *Porte Thiers* and leaving by the *Porte Saint-Roch*; the fourth day from the Porte *de l'Imbert* at four o'clock to the *Porte Saint-Dominique* at ten o'clock; the fifth day from *Portail Magnanen* at five o'clock to the *Porte de l'Oulle* at eleven o'clock; the seventh day from the *Porte de la Ligne* at seven o'clock to the *Porte de la Ligne* at one o'clock; and so on, until on the twenty-fifth day (twenty-fifth because at midnight on the twelfth day he would enter the town through the *Porte du Rhône* and leave it at six o'clock on the thirteenth day by the *Porte Saint-Michel*, and so would only be able to reenter it on the fourteenth day at one in the morning by the *Porte de Ligne*), on the afternoon of the twenty-fifth day, he would enter the town through the *Porte du Rhône* and leave it at six in the evening by the *Porte Saint-Michel*. (On the other hand, this system is so rigid that it might work better if revised and diluted, for example by stipulating that no town gate may be used at any of the times of day originally associated with it: so that at eight A.M. or P.M., for example, any gate could be used except for the *Porte Saint-Charles*, and at two A.M. or two P.M., the *Porte Saint-Lazare* could no longer be used, etc.) For the first few weeks he will have to behave like an undercover agent, like a spy for the secretly mobilized army of a very foreign power. For that period he will have to abandon every fixed habit—sometimes a town is dead before anyone knows it, and by the time you've realized, it's too late, and you find yourself fused through all kinds of innocent habits as if by cells and tissues and capillaries to a complex body in an advanced state of calcification or decomposition. The use of Avignon—like the use of a tool. He will likely devote more attention to unknown, inconsequential streets and squares—

Rue de l'Observance, Rue Crémade, Rue d'Annanelle, Place du Corps-Saint, Rue de l'Aiguarden, Place des Trois Pilats—than to well-known ones: there's a good chance that they are the most significant. During those first weeks he will not expressly seek contact with the people of the town; on the other hand, he will also carefully avoid making a shy, self-absorbed impression on those people whose company he cannot avoid without provoking resentment or suspicion. In fact, he will have most of all to be an apprentice topographer during those three weeks, an observer and as it were a purely haptic explorer of a very large object composed of earth, plants, and all kinds of building materials: what this will boil down to then is that words like *le coin de la Rue des Infirmières et de la Rue Palaphernerie* should evoke for him as soon as possible a concrete image and a series of purposeful movements. Consequently for the time being he will enter only neutral buildings, which do not bring him into that all too compelling contact with the people of now and of the past: cafés, restaurants, the post office, the station, the prefecture if there's a pretext, if need be the theater.

But then the time will come when he is ripe for the real, integrated Avignon. He will move in; preferably into rooms truly affected by the life of the town rather than another hotel immunized with cosmopolitan hygiene. On the day of this new advent he will again walk around the town, but this time on the inside of the walls: *Rue du Rempart Thiers, Rue du Rempart l'Imbert, du Rempart Saint-Michel, du Rempart Saint-Roch, du Rempart de l'Oulle, du Rempart du Rhône.* (And how reasonable it would be to explain his leaving Villeneuve by pointing to the existence of a woman on the opposite bank—but this is as much as it's safe to suggest, lest that unknown woman be reduced in advance to some symbolic, utilitarian, or even commercial object.) But he will still avoid settling in Avignon; his room will remain as impersonal and empty as that of a traveling salesman, since every form of settling-in threatens to dull his necessary receptivity. He will now observe the vital signs of this enormous body more closely than any doctor, any physiologist: nutrition, absorption, blood-cell production, digestion, sleep patterns, peristalsis and retroperistalsis, heartbeat and circulation, all types of breathing—on a daily, weekly, monthly, annual, indefinite basis. He will investigate the daily routine of tradesmen—tailors, cobblers, mechanics, plumbers, painters, electricians, hairdressers, carpenters—merchants—grocers, jewelers, butchers, chemists, wine and book and poultry and antique and furniture dealers—the bank staff, saleswomen in the department store (*Prisunic?*) on the *Rue de la République* just after the *Rue Aubanel*, the clerks at the *Préfecture*, the *Hôtel de Ville*, and the *Caisse d'Epargne*; he will investigate the schedules at the *Lycée* on the *Rue de la République*, the *Lycée des Jeunes Fillles* on the corner of *Rue Palaphernerie* and the *Rue Saint-Joseph*, the *Collège Saint-Joseph* near the *Chapelle des Pénitents Gris*, the *Ecoles des Beaux-Arts* in the *Rue des Lices*, the *Ecole Nationale de Musique* in the *Place du Palais*; the rhythm of the *Pont Saint-Pierre*, the station, the museums, the town library if there is one, the courts of law, the post office, and the quays of the Rhone. He will have to spy on the barracks from outside: *Caserne Saint-Roch* on the *Boulevard Estienne d'Orves*, *Caserne d'Hautpoul* on the *Cours Jean Jaurès*, *Caserne Chabrand* on the *Boulevard Pierre Brossolette*; likewise the fire station in the *Rue Carréterie*, and also any monasteries and the *Hospice Saint-Louis* on the *Rue des Vieilles Etudes*; as far as the *Hôtel-Dieu* is concerned at the *Porte Saint-Lazare*, it would be useful if he could contract a not too serious illness that would allow him to observe hospital life from within; and why not also wish him similar grounds for doing the same at the prison, to the east of the *Promenade du Rocher des Doms*? He will also observe the life of the squares, parks, and public gardens: *Square Agricol Perdiguier*, *Promenade du Rocher des Doms*, and others too, visible on the map but nameless: between the *Rue Pasteur*, the *Rue Joseph Brun*, and the *Rue Charrue*; between the *Rue Paul Manivet*, the *Rue du Rempart Saint-Michel*, and the *Rue Portail Magnanen*; around the PTT building; in the *Rue du Rempart Saint-Roch*; on the corner of the *Rue Velouterie* and the *Boulevard Raspail*; between the *Rue Velouterie* and the *Rempart Saint-Dominique*; in the *Rue Porte Evèque*. He will seek out the plants, factories, and workshops, and, for example, find out whether Avignon still produces—as stated in the *Larousse Illustré* of 1926—silk, madder, and saffron. He will look at the gasworks abandoned on the *Porte Saint-Charles*, and seek out the pumping stations and the waterworks and the power station—unless the town gets its electricity from Donzère-Mondragon? In particular he will discover where and how those employed in such places live. And he will have to visit the cemetery—which not coincidentally is located just to the east of the *Hôtel-Dieu*—and among other things examine the means the rich have used to distinguish their graves from those of the poor. He will observe life in and around the low-rent housing projects—for example, on the *Route de Marseille*—and he will discover whether the rich bourgeois still live in the town—for example, on the *Boulevard Raspail*—or else in what suburbs. He will look in on the abattoir at *Porte Saint-Roch* during working hours, and find out where the animals for slaughter come from. He will often be around the *Halles*, looking to see where the produce they sell there originates, and also who buys it; and then after the market closes he definitely won't have to wait long for the garbage men to come, he'll follow them to the dump, and undoubtedly make interesting discoveries there too. Other markets will also attract his attention, including the stalls that one sometimes finds on the *Boulevard Gabriel Péri*, and perhaps elsewhere too, along the walls, and then the modern vegetable market on the *Route de Marseille*—although this is perhaps less of a market than a shipping station from where the trucks and trains from Cavaillon and elsewhere loaded with fresh produce depart; he will investigate whether the docks to the east of the *Caserne Saint-Roch* and the *Palais de la Foire du Printemps* are markets or storage depots. He will call in regularly at the churches, the synagogue, and the Protestant temple, and decide whether the visitors to each differ—also, those visiting the various Catholic churches, and likewise those attending various services in the same church. He will find out how the people of the town spend the weekends, whether many of them have a weekend cottage, villa, or cabin somewhere out of town—this will require visits to surrounding villages like Noves, Gordes, Pernes-les-Fontaines, Remoulins; he will also ascertain whether there are still people who own large estates and keep a pied-à-terre in Avignon. He will establish contact with people who spend hot evenings on the terraces of the *Place Clémenceau*, and try to form an idea of the composition of this inactive nocturnal population. He will establish what role is played in the annual festival by the inhabitants of Avignon themselves. He will form a picture of the provenance of tourists and the different times of year they pick to visit Avignon; perhaps for this purpose he will take work for a time as an interpreter or night porter in a hotel? One wonders whether a whole lifetime would be enough to really see this town. To see it with the eyes of a stranger, but also with those of a native shopkeeper, a bum, a housekeeper, a farmer and soldier, a priest and poet and patient and day-laborer and whore and journalist and concerned citizen and street sweeper . . . And with the eyes of all the dead, the vagabonds and popes, clerks and troubadours, *fratres minores*, prelates, goliards, painters, bankers, and truck drivers. He will also, if necessary with the help of books, thoroughly explore the city's entire past: in imagination erase the whole town except for the *Rocher des Doms* and the still intact *Pont Saint-Bénezet*; go in search of the remnants of earlier walls; in his mind restore the *Ancien Archevêché*, the *Ancien Couvent des Célestins*, and the *Ancienne Eglise des Cordeliers*; check up on the origins of every street name—*Rue Sureau, Rue Velouterie, Rue du Bon Martinet, Rue du Limas*; see the *Annexe de la Préfecture* in the *Rue Porte Evêque* as the former great seminary, and the *Musée Lapidaire* as the chapel of the lyceum in 1600 or so, and the *Musée Calvet* as the *Hôtel de Villeneuve-Martignan*. (And then there won't be a single excuse remaining for not entering the *Palais des Papes*, the *Palais Vieux*, and the *Palais Nouveau*, the *Salle du Consistoire* and the *Chambre du Cerf*, the chapels inside the *Tour Saint-Jean*, the *Chambre du Parement* and the *Tour des Anges* and the *Grand Tinel*—no valid pretext except perhaps a fear bordering on madness that amid the tourists trotting so innocently and safely after their guide he will be singled out as a man who knows too much, the conspirator who's talked, the spy who has betrayed himself because of his extraordinary attention, and then find himself separated imperceptibly from the touchingly bourgeois, safe herd at one of those moments of disorientation which such an immense and intricate building must offer in abundance, and from that moment on be cut off irrevocably from the world of living human beings outside.) But then there is no reason at all not to extend this exploration further in time, into the future: He will examine the present-day streets with the eyes of the brilliant property speculator, the utopian town planner, and in the most insignificant buildings he will see the construction to come, which they will be demolished to make room for, constructions like the stars whose light has not yet reached the earth. And then the question arises of whether Avignon can survive all this. Whether such an interaction, such intercourse, must not necessarily result in the birth of something new. Whether his arrival can ever be made ultimate other than by his own demise.

January–October 1967

Author's Note to the Original Edition

Was the beginning really as imprecise, as naïve, as ill-considered as I imagine? To be on the safe side, I checked in the diary. Imprecise: ". . . Prose in which the characters would be *objects*: a whole town just the same as the most trifling urban object. In the same way that in an ordinary novel the characters are linked by the plot, these objects would be linked by people." (11-16-66) Naïve: "Because I have a clear idea of what I want to achieve in terms of these objects." (01-07-67) Ill-considered: "Off we go then. The less one thinks off the paper, the better." (01-09) The primary aim was actually to devote words to the object called Avignon, to bombard the name Avignon, as it were, with words in a literary cyclotron. There were plenty of surprises. And factually at least Avignon must be less arbitrary for me than, say, Prague, where I've never set foot—yet more arbitrary than my hometown. And probably *every* object that we make room for in our life immediately structures that life—the important thing, don't you agree, is to actually acknowledge and experience this fact.

Suivez le guide: I invite you to follow the (spiral-shaped) path that I describe for you here.

d.r.

May 1969

p. 11

Avignon, 29 septembre 1843 . . . Le pays que je parcours est admirable . . . il est impossible de voir un pays qui ressemble plus à l'Espagne. L'aspect du paysage et de la ville est le même. Les ouvriers se couchent à l'ombre ou se drapent de leurs manteaux d'un air aussi tragique que les Andalous. Partout l'odeur d'ail et d'huile se marie à celle des oranges et du jasmin. Les rues sont couvertes de toiles pendant le jour, et les femmes ont de petits pieds bien chaussés. Il n'y a pas jusqu'au patois qui n'ait de loin le son de l'espagnol. Un plus grand rapport se trouve encore produit par l'abondance des cousins, puces, punaises, qui ne permettent pas de dormir . . .

p. 14

L'armée royale s'arrête devant Avignon qui, après avoir protesté de son obéissance, lui refuse le passage; le roi, "pour venger l'injure faite à l'armée du Christ," prête le serment de ne pas bouger de place avant d'avoir pris la ville et fait dresser les machines de guerre. Le premier effroi passé, Avignon est decidée à tenir. De plus, ville d'Empire, elle n'entend pas se laisser faire la loi par le roi de France. Les murs de la ville sont solides et défendus par une milice nombreuse et une forte garnison de routiers. Avignon se défendit si énergiquement que pendant deux mois on put hésiter sur l'issue de la guerre. Mais pendant que les soldats étaient exposés à la faim, aux épidémies, aux flèches et aux boulets des assiégés et aux attaques des armées du comte de Toulouse qui harcelaient les arrières de l'armée royale, le roi recevait les deputations des seigneurs et des villes du Midi que la présence des croisés et la crainte de nouveaux massacres incitaient à la soumisssion . . .

pp. 22–23

Ist es möglich, dass man noch nichts Wirkliches und Wichtiges gesehen, erkannt und gesagt hat? Ist es möglich, dass man Jahrtausende Zeit gehabt hat, zu schauen, nachzudenken und aufzuzeichen, und dass man die Jahrtausende hat vergehen lassen wie eine Schulpause, in der man sein Butterbrot isst und einen Apfel?—Ja, es ist möglich.—Ist es möglich, dass man trotz Erfindungen und Fortschritten, trotz Kultur, Religion und Weltweisheit an der Oberfläche des Lebens geblieben ist? Ist es möglich, dass man sogar diese Oberfläche, die doch immerhin etwas gewesen ware, mit einem unglaublich langweiligen Stoff überzogen hat, so dass sie aussieht wie die Salonmöbel in den Sommerferien?—Ja, es ist möglich.

p. 30
L'amoureux est toujours craintif. A la vue soudaine de son amante, le cœur d'un amant doit tressaillir. Tout amant doit pâlir en présence de son amante.

p. 43
Es waren die Tage jener avignonesischen Christenheit, die sich vor einem Menschenalter um Johann den Zweiundzwanzigsten zusammengezogen hatte, mit so viel unwillkürlicher Zuflucht, dass an dem Platze seines Pontifikats, gleich nach ihm, die Masse dieses Palastes entstanden war, verschlossen und schwer wie ein äusserster Notleib für die wohnlose Seele aller.

pp. 64–65
Avignon leur envoie des messagers et, dès qu'ils se présentent devant la ville, une délégation de seigneurs et de bourgeois les reçoit à genoux, et leur offre la ville. 'Sire comte de Saint-Gilles, dit le chef de cette délégation, vous et votre

bien-aimé fils, de notre lignée, acceptez cet honorable gage: tout Avignon se met en votre seigneurie: chacun vous livre sa personne et ses biens, les clefs de la ville, les jardins et les portes, etc." Le comte félicite les Avignonnais de leur accueil et leur promet "l'estime de toute la chrétienté et de votre pays, car vous restaurez les preux, et Joie et Parage."—Le père et le fils entrent dans la ville. "Il n'y a vieillard ni jouvenceau qui n'accoure tout joyeux à travers les rues. Il se tient pour fortuné, celui qui peut courir le mieux! Les uns crient: 'Toulouse!' en l'honneur du père et du fils, et les autres: 'Joie! Désormais Dieu sera avec nous!'"

pp. 68–69
En ce temps, avoit en ung bois sur le Rhône, entre Arles et Avignon, ung dragon demy beste et demy poisson plus gros que ung beuf et plus long que ung cheval; et avoit les dens agues comme une espée, et estoit cornu des deux costez. Si ce tapissoit en l'eau, tuoit les poissons et noyoit les nefz; . . . Ce dragon estoit appellé du pays, Tarascon . . .

p. 98
Le sillon rhodanien est la seule percée naturelle qui fasse communiquer en Occident l'Europe du Nord et l'Europe du Midi: il constituait à l'aube du XIVe-siècle la voie axiale du trafic entre les deux centres économiques les plus évolués de la chrétienté,

l'Italie centrale et septentrionale d'une part, la Flandre de l'autre, et entre les centres politiques les plus importants, Londres et Paris au nord, Rome et Naples au sud . . . Située à 150 km au sud de Vienne . . . Avignon n'impose pas un crochet vers le nord aux voyageurs qui, venus de l'Italie, entendent se rendre en Languedoc, en Aquitaine ou en Espagne sans rupture de charge et sans embarquement, et surtout . . . elle est plus proche de la mer. Sur son fameux pont Saint-Bénezet, dont la construction de 1177 à 1185 a laissé le souvenir d'un prodige, l'ancienne via Domitia franchit le Rhône depuis la destruction du pont romain à Arles; et comme le pont d'Avignon est le dernier des ponts jetés sur le Rhône avant son embouchure, la ville est en situation de bénéficier de quelquesuns des avantages des ports d'estuaire . . .

p. 100

. . . Fast täglich, während siebzehn Tagen, hab ich den immensen Papstpalast gesehen, diese hermetisch verschlossene Burg, in der die Papstschaft, da sie sich am Rande anfaulen fühlte, sich zu konservieren gedachte, sich selber einkochend in einer letzten Leidenschaft. Sooft man dieses verzweifelte Haus auch wiedersieht, es steht auf einem Felsen von Unwahrscheinlichkeit, und man kommt nur hinein mit einem Sprung über alles Bisherige und Glaubhafte.

p. 106

. . . und da schrieen sie ihn an. Ganz Europa schrie: dieser Glaube war schlecht.

p. 115

Avignon est rempli d'églises et de palais, tous munis de hautes tours avec créneaux et machicoulis. Le palais des papes est un modèle de fortification pour le moyen âge. Cela prouve quelle aimable sécurité régnait dans ce pays vers le XIIe- ou XIVe-siècle . . . Les Avignonnais sont aussi fiers de leur inquisition que les Anglais de leur Magna Charta. "Nous aussi, disent-ils, nous avons eu des auto-da-fé, et les Espagnols n'en ont eu qu'après nous!"

p. 115

In den hübschen Anlagen hinter dem alten Palast der Päpste in Avignon steht eine Aussichtsbank, von der man über die Rhone, über das Blumenufer der Durance, über Höhen und Fluren und über einem Teil der Stadt hinaussieht.

p. 115

La vue sur les riches berges du Rhône est superbe du haut des jardins qui entourent le vieux Palais des Papes en Avignon.

*

p. 115

Vom anderen Rhoneufer, van Villeneuve gesehen, liess mich die Stadt, Gott weiss warum, an Nowgorod, den grossen, denken . . .

p. 117

Ici le Rhône a dépassé la côte d'alerte, mais à cause des pompes spéciales qui ont été mises en action, pour éviter l'inondation des bas quartiers de la ville, il s'est contenté de recouvrir les allées de l'Oulle et l'île de la Barthelasse (île située entre le bras du Rhône vif et du Rhône mort) . . .

pp. 120–121

10 Septembre 1843 . . . Dans le palais des papes, on monte une centaine de marches d'un escalier tortueux, puis tout à coup on se trouve vis-à-vis une muraille. En tournant la tête, on voit, à quinze pieds plus haut, la continuation de l'escalier, où l'on ne peut parvenir que par une échelle. Il y a aussi des chambres souterraines qui servaient à l'inquisition. On montre les fourneaux où l'on chauffait les ferrements pour torturer les hérétiques, et les débris d'une machine très-compliquée pour donner la question . . . —Gebete und Verwünschungen, Segen und Bannfluch in Ohr, wandeln wir hinter dem Führer, der uns seinen eingetrichterten Text aufsagt, durch die labyrintisch verzweigten Flügel des Doppelpalastes, der trotz seiner uneinheitlichen Anlage durch die Wucht seiner Baumasse wirkt wie aus einem Guss, über hallende Höfe in kirchweite Säle, durch

herrlich bemalte Gemächer, Kapellen, Sakristeien, Turmzimmer, durch verborgene Gänge un schmalüberwölbte Galereien, über Treppen, wie von Maulwürfen durch die Dicke der Mauern gegraben, in Küchen, deren Kamine einen ganzen Ochsen aufnehmen konnten, kurz verweilend an schwindelnd hohen Fenstern und auf Terrassen, von denen der Blick hinabfällt ins graue Gewirr der Gassen und Plätze, schliesslich über eine letzte Treppe wieder hinunter in den Hof, der uns ängstigt mit seinen riesigen Ausmassen.

DANIËL ROBBERECHTS (1937–1992) is best remembered for his two works of autobiographical prose, each centered on a particular city, and now considered classics of Flemish literature: *Arriving in Avignon* and *Writing Prague*. At the time of his death, he was engaged in a ten-volume project investigating the manipulative mechanisms of language.

PAUL VINCENT is an award-winning translator of Dutch literature whose translation of Hendrik Marsman's *Herinnering aan Holland* earned the David Reid Poetry Translation Prize.

PETROS ABATZOGLOU, *What Does Mrs. Freeman Want?*
MICHAL AJVAZ, *The Golden Age.*
The Other City.
PIERRE ALBERT-BIROT, *Grabinoulor.*
YUZ ALESHKOVSKY, *Kangaroo.*
FELIPE ALFAU, *Chromos.*
Locos.
IVAN ÂNGELO, *The Celebration.*
The Tower of Glass.
DAVID ANTIN, *Talking.*
ANTÓNIO LOBO ANTUNES, *Knowledge of Hell.*
ALAIN ARIAS-MISSON, *Theatre of Incest.*
IFTIKHAR ARIF AND WAQAS KHWAJA, EDS., *Modern Poetry of Pakistan.*
JOHN ASHBERY AND JAMES SCHUYLER, *A Nest of Ninnies.*
HEIMRAD BÄCKER, *transcript.*
DJUNA BARNES, *Ladies Almanack.*
Ryder.
JOHN BARTH, *LETTERS.*
Sabbatical.
DONALD BARTHELME, *The King.*
Paradise.
SVETISLAV BASARA, *Chinese Letter.*
RENÉ BELLETTO, *Dying.*
MARK BINELLI, *Sacco and Vanzetti Must Die!*
ANDREI BITOV, *Pushkin House.*
ANDREJ BLATNIK, *You Do Understand.*
LOUIS PAUL BOON, *Chapel Road.*
My Little War.
Summer in Termuren.
ROGER BOYLAN, *Killoyle.*
IGNÁCIO DE LOYOLA BRANDÃO, *Anonymous Celebrity.*
The Good-Bye Angel.
Teeth under the Sun.
Zero.
BONNIE BREMSER, *Troia: Mexican Memoirs.*
CHRISTINE BROOKE-ROSE, *Amalgamemnon.*
BRIGID BROPHY, *In Transit.*
MEREDITH BROSNAN, *Mr. Dynamite.*
GERALD L. BRUNS, *Modern Poetry and the Idea of Language.*
EVGENY BUNIMOVICH AND J. KATES, EDS., *Contemporary Russian Poetry: An Anthology.*
GABRIELLE BURTON, *Heartbreak Hotel.*
MICHEL BUTOR, *Degrees.*
Mobile.
Portrait of the Artist as a Young Ape.
G. CABRERA INFANTE, *Infante's Inferno.*
Three Trapped Tigers.
JULIETA CAMPOS, *The Fear of Losing Eurydice.*
ANNE CARSON, *Eros the Bittersweet.*
ORLY CASTEL-BLOOM, *Dolly City.*
CAMILO JOSÉ CELA, *Christ versus Arizona.*
The Family of Pascual Duarte.
The Hive.
LOUIS-FERDINAND CÉLINE, *Castle to Castle.*
Conversations with Professor Y.
London Bridge.

Normance.
North.
Rigadoon.
HUGO CHARTERIS, *The Tide Is Right.*
JEROME CHARYN, *The Tar Baby.*
MARC CHOLODENKO, *Mordechai Schamz.*
JOSHUA COHEN, *Witz.*
EMILY HOLMES COLEMAN, *The Shutter of Snow.*
ROBERT COOVER, *A Night at the Movies.*
STANLEY CRAWFORD, *Log of the S.S. The Mrs Unguentine.*
Some Instructions to My Wife.
ROBERT CREELEY, *Collected Prose.*
RENÉ CREVEL, *Putting My Foot in It.*
RALPH CUSACK, *Cadenza.*
SUSAN DAITCH, *L.C.*
Storytown.
NICHOLAS DELBANCO, *The Count of Concord.*
NIGEL DENNIS, *Cards of Identity.*
PETER DIMOCK, *A Short Rhetoric for Leaving the Family.*
ARIEL DORFMAN, *Konfidenz.*
COLEMAN DOWELL, *The Houses of Children.*
Island People.
Too Much Flesh and Jabez.
ARKADII DRAGOMOSHCHENKO, *Dust.*
RIKKI DUCORNET, *The Complete Butcher's Tales.*
The Fountains of Neptune.
The Jade Cabinet.
The One Marvelous Thing.
Phosphor in Dreamland.
The Stain.
The Word "Desire."
WILLIAM EASTLAKE, *The Bamboo Bed.*
Castle Keep.
Lyric of the Circle Heart.
JEAN ECHENOZ, *Chopin's Move.*
STANLEY ELKIN, *A Bad Man.*
Boswell: A Modern Comedy.
Criers and Kibitzers, Kibitzers and Criers.
The Dick Gibson Show.
The Franchiser.
George Mills.
The Living End.
The MacGuffin.
The Magic Kingdom.
Mrs. Ted Bliss.
The Rabbi of Lud.
Van Gogh's Room at Arles.
ANNIE ERNAUX, *Cleaned Out.*
LAUREN FAIRBANKS, *Muzzle Thyself.*
Sister Carrie.
LESLIE A. FIEDLER, *Love and Death in the American Novel.*
JUAN FILLOY, *Op Oloop.*
GUSTAVE FLAUBERT, *Bouvard and Pécuchet.*
KASS FLEISHER, *Talking out of School.*
FORD MADOX FORD, *The March of Literature.*
JON FOSSE, *Aliss at the Fire.*
Melancholy.

MAX FRISCH, *I'm Not Stiller.*
Man in the Holocene.
CARLOS FUENTES, *Christopher Unborn.*
Distant Relations.
Terra Nostra.
Where the Air Is Clear.
JANICE GALLOWAY, *Foreign Parts.*
The Trick Is to Keep Breathing.
WILLIAM H. GASS, *Cartesian Sonata and Other Novellas.*
Finding a Form.
A Temple of Texts.
The Tunnel.
Willie Masters' Lonesome Wife.
GÉRARD GAVARRY, *Hoppla! 1 2 3.*
ETIENNE GILSON,
The Arts of the Beautiful.
Forms and Substances in the Arts.
C. S. GISCOMBE, *Giscome Road.*
Here.
Prairie Style.
DOUGLAS GLOVER, *Bad News of the Heart.*
The Enamoured Knight.
WITOLD GOMBROWICZ,
A Kind of Testament.
KAREN ELIZABETH GORDON,
The Red Shoes.
GEORGI GOSPODINOV, *Natural Novel.*
JUAN GOYTISOLO, *Count Julian.*
Juan the Landless.
Makbara.
Marks of Identity.
PATRICK GRAINVILLE, *The Cave of Heaven.*
HENRY GREEN, *Back.*
Blindness.
Concluding.
Doting.
Nothing.
JIŘÍ GRUŠA, *The Questionnaire.*
GABRIEL GUDDING,
Rhode Island Notebook.
MELA HARTWIG, *Am I a Redundant Human Being?*
JOHN HAWKES, *The Passion Artist.*
Whistlejacket.
ALEKSANDAR HEMON, ED.,
Best European Fiction.
AIDAN HIGGINS, *A Bestiary.*
Balcony of Europe.
Bornholm Night-Ferry.
Darkling Plain: Texts for the Air.
Flotsam and Jetsam.
Langrishe, Go Down.
Scenes from a Receding Past.
Windy Arbours.
KEIZO HINO, *Isle of Dreams.*
ALDOUS HUXLEY, *Antic Hay.*
Crome Yellow.
Point Counter Point.
Those Barren Leaves.
Time Must Have a Stop.
MIKHAIL IOSSEL AND JEFF PARKER, EDS.,
Amerika: Russian Writers View the United States.
GERT JONKE, *The Distant Sound.*
Geometric Regional Novel.

Homage to Czerny.
The System of Vienna.
JACQUES JOUET, *Mountain R.*
Savage.
CHARLES JULIET, *Conversations with Samuel Beckett and Bram van Velde.*
MIEKO KANAI, *The Word Book.*
YORAM KANIUK, *Life on Sandpaper.*
HUGH KENNER, *The Counterfeiters.*
Flaubert, Joyce and Beckett: The Stoic Comedians.
Joyce's Voices.
DANILO KIŠ, *Garden, Ashes.*
A Tomb for Boris Davidovich.
ANITA KONKKA, *A Fool's Paradise.*
GEORGE KONRÁD, *The City Builder.*
TADEUSZ KONWICKI, *A Minor Apocalypse.*
The Polish Complex.
MENIS KOUMANDAREAS, *Koula.*
ELAINE KRAF, *The Princess of 72nd Street.*
JIM KRUSOE, *Iceland.*
EWA KURYLUK, *Century 21.*
EMILIO LASCANO TEGUI, *On Elegance While Sleeping.*
ERIC LAURRENT, *Do Not Touch.*
VIOLETTE LEDUC, *La Bâtarde.*
SUZANNE JILL LEVINE, *The Subversive Scribe: Translating Latin American Fiction.*
DEBORAH LEVY, *Billy and Girl.*
Pillow Talk in Europe and Other Places.
JOSÉ LEZAMA LIMA, *Paradiso.*
ROSA LIKSOM, *Dark Paradise.*
OSMAN LINS, *Avalovara.*
The Queen of the Prisons of Greece.
ALF MAC LOCHLAINN,
The Corpus in the Library.
Out of Focus.
RON LOEWINSOHN, *Magnetic Field(s).*
BRIAN LYNCH, *The Winner of Sorrow.*
D. KEITH MANO, *Take Five.*
MICHELINE AHARONIAN MARCOM,
The Mirror in the Well.
BEN MARCUS,
The Age of Wire and String.
WALLACE MARKFIELD,
Teitlebaum's Window.
To an Early Grave.
DAVID MARKSON, *Reader's Block.*
Springer's Progress.
Wittgenstein's Mistress.
CAROLE MASO, *AVA.*
LADISLAV MATEJKA AND KRYSTYNA POMORSKA, EDS.,
Readings in Russian Poetics: Formalist and Structuralist Views.
HARRY MATHEWS,
The Case of the Persevering Maltese: Collected Essays.
Cigarettes.
The Conversions.
The Human Country: New and Collected Stories.
The Journalist.

My Life in CIA.
Singular Pleasures.
The Sinking of the Odradek
  Stadium.
Tlooth.
20 Lines a Day.
JOSEPH MCELROY,
  Night Soul and Other Stories.
ROBERT L. MCLAUGHLIN, ED.,
  Innovations: An Anthology of
  Modern & Contemporary Fiction.
HERMAN MELVILLE, *The Confidence-Man.*
AMANDA MICHALOPOULOU, *I'd Like.*
STEVEN MILLHAUSER,
  The Barnum Museum.
  In the Penny Arcade.
RALPH J. MILLS, JR.,
  Essays on Poetry.
MOMUS, *The Book of Jokes.*
CHRISTINE MONTALBETTI, *Western.*
OLIVE MOORE, *Spleen.*
NICHOLAS MOSLEY, *Accident.*
  Assassins.
  Catastrophe Practice.
  Children of Darkness and Light.
  Experience and Religion.
  God's Hazard.
  The Hesperides Tree.
  Hopeful Monsters.
  Imago Bird.
  Impossible Object.
  Inventing God.
  Judith.
  Look at the Dark.
  Natalie Natalia.
  Paradoxes of Peace.
  Serpent.
  Time at War.
  The Uses of Slime Mould:
    Essays of Four Decades.
WARREN MOTTE,
  Fables of the Novel: French Fiction
    since 1990.
  Fiction Now: The French Novel in
    the 21st Century.
  Oulipo: A Primer of Potential
    Literature.
YVES NAVARRE, *Our Share of Time.*
  Sweet Tooth.
DOROTHY NELSON, *In Night's City.*
  Tar and Feathers.
ESHKOL NEVO, *Homesick.*
WILFRIDO D. NOLLEDO,
  But for the Lovers.
FLANN O'BRIEN,
  At Swim-Two-Birds.
  At War.
  The Best of Myles.
  The Dalkey Archive.
  Further Cuttings.
  The Hard Life.
  The Poor Mouth.
  The Third Policeman.
CLAUDE OLLIER, *The Mise-en-Scène.*
PATRIK OUŘEDNÍK, *Europeana.*
BORIS PAHOR, *Necropolis.*

FERNANDO DEL PASO,
  News from the Empire.
  Palinuro of Mexico.
ROBERT PINGET, *The Inquisitory.*
  Mahu or The Material.
  Trio.
MANUEL PUIG,
  Betrayed by Rita Hayworth.
  The Buenos Aires Affair.
  Heartbreak Tango.
RAYMOND QUENEAU, *The Last Days.*
  Odile.
  Pierrot Mon Ami.
  Saint Glinglin.
ANN QUIN, *Berg.*
  Passages.
  Three.
  Tripticks.
ISHMAEL REED,
  The Free-Lance Pallbearers.
  The Last Days of Louisiana Red.
  Ishmael Reed: The Plays.
  Reckless Eyeballing.
  The Terrible Threes.
  The Terrible Twos.
  Yellow Back Radio Broke-Down.
JEAN RICARDOU, *Place Names.*
RAINER MARIA RILKE, *The Notebooks of*
  Malte Laurids Brigge.
JULIÁN RÍOS, *The House of Ulysses.*
  Larva: A Midsummer Night's Babel.
  Poundemonium.
AUGUSTO ROA BASTOS, *I the Supreme.*
DANIËL ROBBERECHTS,
  Arriving in Avignon.
OLIVIER ROLIN, *Hotel Crystal.*
ALIX CLEO ROUBAUD, *Alix's Journal.*
JACQUES ROUBAUD, *The Form of a*
  City Changes Faster, Alas, Than
  the Human Heart.
  The Great Fire of London.
  Hortense in Exile.
  Hortense Is Abducted.
  The Loop.
  The Plurality of Worlds of Lewis.
  The Princess Hoppy.
  Some Thing Black.
LEON S. ROUDIEZ,
  French Fiction Revisited.
VEDRANA RUDAN, *Night.*
STIG SÆTERBAKKEN, *Siamese.*
LYDIE SALVAYRE, *The Company of Ghosts.*
  Everyday Life.
  The Lecture.
  Portrait of the Writer as a
    Domesticated Animal.
  The Power of Flies.
LUIS RAFAEL SÁNCHEZ,
  Macho Camacho's Beat.
SEVERO SARDUY, *Cobra & Maitreya.*
NATHALIE SARRAUTE,
  Do You Hear Them?
  Martereau.
  The Planetarium.
ARNO SCHMIDT, *Collected Stories.*
  Nobodaddy's Children.

FOR A FULL LIST OF PUBLICATIONS, VISIT:
www.dalkeyarchive.com

CHRISTINE SCHUTT, *Nightwork*.
GAIL SCOTT, *My Paris*.
DAMION SEARLS, *What We Were Doing and Where We Were Going*.
JUNE AKERS SEESE,
Is This What Other Women Feel Too?
What Waiting Really Means.
BERNARD SHARE, *Inish*.
Transit.
AURELIE SHEEHAN,
Jack Kerouac Is Pregnant.
VIKTOR SHKLOVSKY, *Knight's Move*.
A Sentimental Journey:
Memoirs 1917–1922.
Energy of Delusion: A Book on Plot.
Literature and Cinematography.
Theory of Prose.
Third Factory.
Zoo, or Letters Not about Love.
CLAUDE SIMON, *The Invitation*.
PIERRE SINIAC, *The Collaborators*.
JOSEF ŠKVORECKÝ, *The Engineer of Human Souls*.
GILBERT SORRENTINO,
Aberration of Starlight.
Blue Pastoral.
Crystal Vision.
Imaginative Qualities of Actual Things.
Mulligan Stew.
Pack of Lies.
Red the Fiend.
The Sky Changes.
Something Said.
Splendide-Hôtel.
Steelwork.
Under the Shadow.
W. M. SPACKMAN,
The Complete Fiction.
ANDRZEJ STASIUK, *Fado*.
GERTRUDE STEIN,
Lucy Church Amiably.
The Making of Americans.
A Novel of Thank You.
LARS SVENDSEN, *A Philosophy of Evil*.
PIOTR SZEWC, *Annihilation*.
GONÇALO M. TAVARES, *Jerusalem*.
LUCIAN DAN TEODOROVICI,
Our Circus Presents . . .
STEFAN THEMERSON, *Hobson's Island*.
The Mystery of the Sardine.
Tom Harris.
JOHN TOOMEY, *Sleepwalker*.
JEAN-PHILIPPE TOUSSAINT,
The Bathroom.
Camera.
Monsieur.
Running Away.
Self-Portrait Abroad.
Television.
DUMITRU TSEPENEAG,
Hotel Europa.
The Necessary Marriage.
Pigeon Post.
Vain Art of the Fugue.
ESTHER TUSQUETS, *Stranded*.

DUBRAVKA UGRESIC,
Lend Me Your Character.
Thank You for Not Reading.
MATI UNT, *Brecht at Night*.
Diary of a Blood Donor.
Things in the Night.
ÁLVARO URIBE AND OLIVIA SEARS, EDS.,
Best of Contemporary Mexican Fiction.
ELOY URROZ, *Friction*.
The Obstacles.
LUISA VALENZUELA, *He Who Searches*.
MARJA-LIISA VARTIO,
The Parson's Widow.
PAUL VERHAEGHEN, *Omega Minor*.
BORIS VIAN, *Heartsnatcher*.
LLORENÇ VILLALONGA, *The Dolls' Room*.
ORNELA VORPSI, *The Country Where No One Ever Dies*.
AUSTRYN WAINHOUSE, *Hedyphagetica*.
PAUL WEST,
Words for a Deaf Daughter & Gala.
CURTIS WHITE,
America's Magic Mountain.
The Idea of Home.
Memories of My Father Watching TV.
Monstrous Possibility: An Invitation to Literary Politics.
Requiem.
DIANE WILLIAMS, *Excitability:*
Selected Stories.
Romancer Erector.
DOUGLAS WOOLF, *Wall to Wall*.
Ya! & John-Juan.
JAY WRIGHT, *Polynomials and Pollen*.
The Presentable Art of Reading Absence.
PHILIP WYLIE, *Generation of Vipers*.
MARGUERITE YOUNG,
Angel in the Forest.
Miss MacIntosh, My Darling.
REYOUNG, *Unbabbling*.
VLADO ŽABOT, *The Succubus*.
ZORAN ŽIVKOVIĆ, *Hidden Camera*.
LOUIS ZUKOFSKY, *Collected Fiction*.
SCOTT ZWIREN, *God Head*.